AIRSHIP 27 PRODUCTIONS

The Musketeers New Adventures

"The Devil of Monferrato" © 2021 Joel Jenkins
"The Lady of Acadia" © 2021 Paul Beale
"Noblese Oblige" © 2021 Alan J. Porter

Published by Airship 27 Productions
www.airship27.com
www.airship27hangar.com

Interior illustrations© 2021 Ed Catto
Cover illustration © 2021 Adam Shaw

Editor: Ron Fortier
Associate Editor: Gordon Dymowski
Marketing and Promotions Manager: Michael Vance
Production Designer: Rob Davis.

ISBN: 978-1-953589-00-2

Printed in the United States of America

10 9 8 7 6 5 4 3 2 1

Table of Contents

The King's Musketeers are dispatched to Italy to help Duke Nevers fend off an invasion by the Spanish and their German Hapsburg allies.

Musketeer D'Artagnan travels to the new world to witness the battle of Fort Latour in New Brunswick, Canada, and finds himself pitted against a sadistic agent of the Cardinal's known as the Musketeer Killer.

A lost letter written by the Queen must be found or else it threatens a new war with Spain. Desperately she calls upon a retired Musketeer to find the missing message.

The Devil of Monferrato
By Joel Jenkins

hree days since the French hosts, four hundred strong, had violated the Italian border, the Musketeer Porthos shifted his prodigious bulk uncomfortably in his saddle and complained vociferously. "I believe my saddle sores have saddle sores. I fear my sturdy frame is not meant for such miniscule furniture—would that I had not gambled away the most excellent saddle made for me by the estimable Monsieur Sellier. That man is a master at his art."

"Why, I do believe I see your saddle riding by at this very moment," replied the wiry D'Artagnan—the youngest of the Musketeers and one who rode easily enough in his saddle.

Porthos scowled as the magnificently attired Captain of the Heavy Artillerie reached them on the trail and capered his most excellent stallion to a halt.

"Monsieurs," addressed Captain Montagne, "what is the delay? The road must be cleared for the cannons." The Captain gestured to teams of horses struggling to pull artillery pieces up the steep mountain paths. "After all, they are the most critical part of any assault."

"I am merely pausing to enjoy the view from these lofty heights," replied Porthos, mentioning nothing of his saddle sores to Captain Montagne. "From this point I believe I can espy the distant fortress of Casale Monferrato and even see the Spanish dogs who assail our friend the Duke of Nevers."

"Our friend?" scoffed Captain Montagne. "I know not if the Duke of Nevers is a friend. I know only that the King Louis has commanded we come to his aid, and so we come—whether he be friend or no."

Athos was the wisest of the Musketeers—a man of keen intellect, so if any understood the reasons behind the foray into Italy it was him. "The Duke of Nevers is only our friend because he owns some French holdings in Piedmont Savoy. Even so, King Louis and Cardinal Richelieu were reluctant to admit the friendship because they were busy putting down the

Huguenots in La Rochelle."

"My expertise is mathematics," replied Captain Montagne with a shrug of his narrow shoulders. "I am a wizard with gunpowder and trajectory. Those things I understand—"

"And you understand the odds of gambling and cards," interjected the musketeer Aramis, who sat erect and regal in his saddle, fingering a golden cross that lay around his neck, and who had been roused from the reverie of his examination of the enemy forces ranged around the Fortress Casale Monferrato. "And so you were able to take advantage of our poor slow-witted friend, Porthos, who was too amiable to realize you might steal his saddle out from beneath him."

"Admittedly, my mathematical magician-ship makes such gambling feats akin to plucking alms from the chapeau of a blind man," said Captain Montagne, "but I did not cheat! I merely understood and exploited the mathematical possibilities and there is no sin in that."

"No cheating perhaps," replied Aramis, "but I am well acquainted with sin—and it is not my business to absolve you of any wrongdoing against God."

"It is well you acknowledge your own faults," said the incensed Captain Montagne, "but do not accuse me of sin!"

"Then you feel it is no sin to rob a fellow soldier of the very saddle of his horse—a thing that is as important to a musketeer as his sword, or perhaps his own right hand?"

Captain Montagne shifted uncomfortably in his saddle as the truth of Aramis's words stung him. "I would not put the loss of a saddle in such terms."

"Then you will restore the saddle?" pressed Aramis.

"Nay! I won this saddle with all fairness in a game of strategy—and giving back the saddle would be admitting fault in how I had won the prize. And I will admit no such fault!"

"You would not be admitting fault," said Aramis, "but rather you would be displaying your noblesse, magnanimity, and generosity to all."

"And then every slow-witted card player should expect the same generosity," objected Captain Montagne. "And I should be poverty stricken upon returning every ecu and pistole I have ever won!"

Porthos looked on in puzzlement as this debate between his old friend Aramis and Captain Montagne was raging, not quite following the verbal interplay. Every time he was about to interject, either Captain Montagne or Aramis spoke again.

"I speak not of ecu or pistole," said Aramis. "I speak of the very equipment upon which a soldier depends to execute his honorable profession as he has sworn before God and king! Now, I request one final time that you return the saddle to my estimable associate Porthos. You shall not need it when lobbing iron at the Spanish hosts."

"Again, I say that I shall not return what was fairly won. To do so would be to admit wrongdoing—of which I am not guilty, despite your foolish blusterings to the contrary."

Now, Aramis had Captain Montagne where he wanted him. "Then perhaps you will offer us the opportunity to win the saddle back."

This offer intrigued Captain Montagne, for he saw the opportunity to further enrich himself—beyond a mere saddle that was too large for his slender frame, despite all its finery. He would not admit it, but it sat poorly upon his horse, which was too small of stature to support a man of such prodigious size as Porthos, and riding in it made him bow-legged and uncomfortable. "I should be happy to meet you over the card table just as soon as we have prosecuted our victory over the Spanish."

"What I have in mind won't be so needlessly delayed, but you will still be able to employ your scientific wizardry," suggested Aramis.

"Speak on," said Montagne, who was clearly intrigued.

"I wager that my friends and I—the noble Porthos, who you hold in such disdain as to steal his saddle, the young and brave Gascon D'Artagnan, the most excellent Athos, and my own humble self will reach the walls of the fortress of Casale Monferrato before your fusillades of cannon fire disperse the Spanish hosts. If we win you will return to Porthos his saddle and give us one hundred pistoles."

"And if I should win the wager?" questioned Montagne. "What profit is there to entice me to this gamble?"

"You shall win one hundred pistoles," said Aramis.

"But the wager is not even!" objected Montagne. "This saddle that once formerly belonged to Porthos is worth at least twenty pistoles!"

"That's not what you valued it at last night," interjected Porthos, who finally found his tongue. "I believe you estimated it at ten pistoles."

"Since using the saddle, I have taken a liking to it. It's value has risen in my estimation."

"Why, your legs cannot even straddle it!" exclaimed Porthos.

"Very well," conceded Captain Montagne. "I will allow ten pistoles. If I win the wager you shall owe me 110 pistoles!"

"Then we have a bargain!" said Aramis.

"Only if you should clear the way," replied Montagne. "I shall need time to bring my artillery into the foothills around Casale Monferrato and I will not brook any interference from laggard musketeers—and for the life of me, I do not understand why King Louis should send only four of you. It's as if he thinks a mere four men will be sufficient to drive off all the hosts of Spain."

Athos cast a glance in D'Artagnan's direction. "I am sure our paucity of numbers has to do with other reasons."

Porthos found a slightly more comfortable position in his too-small saddle and they resumed their travels over the crest of the mountain pass, clearing the way for the struggling teams drawing the artillery pieces up the steep paths. When they were out of earshot of Montagne, Porthos turned to Aramis.

"Hold a moment, friend Aramis. Did you call me slow-witted, or did my ears deceive me?"

"Surely, your ears have deceived you, loyal friend," replied Aramis.

"I thought they must have," said Porthos.

"My question," said D'Artagnan, "is do we have 110 pistoles between us to pay Captain Montagne if we should lose this wager? I know for myself that my funds are limited to a mere six pistoles, as the expenses of the road have severely depleted my personal wealth."

"I lost every pistole and ecu at cards last evening," lamented Porthos.

"Then my eleven pistoles stands me as the wealthiest of our companionship," estimated Athos, "unless our friend, Aramis, has more wealth hidden in his saddlebags than I suspect."

"I have naught but nine pistoles and a handful of ecus," reported Aramis.

D'Artagnan raised his eyebrows. "And yet you have wagered 110 pistoles…"

"Perhaps," said Aramis, "you recall a wager in which we promised to spend an hour picnicking on the contested Bastions of St. Gervais? If we succeed at our venture we will replenish our rapidly failing funds at the expense of a pompous captain who knows no fear only because he never has to face the enemy but from hundreds of yards distant."

"And I shall have my saddle back!" exclaimed Porthos. "No longer shall I be forced to ride in furniture designed for men of dwarfly stature."

D'Artagnan resigned himself to the idea that losing the wager was no option. "I know why King Louis has relegated us to being the only Musketeers to support this relief to the Duke of Nevers—and for that I apologize. I must admit the charms of Her Excellency are beyond my capability to resist." Briefly, the young Gascon's mind recalled Queen Anne's raven dark hair, olive complexion, and hourglass figure.

"And she seems to have found you charming as well," replied Athos, his expression shrewd and calculating. "Or else we shouldn't have been banished from the kingdom and send to die in a foreign land."

Nor did Porthos fail to comprehend the thrust of the conversation. "It would be a shame for us to have saved the Queen from one scandal only to be the cause of another."

"There is no cause," maintained D'Artagnan, "but the overwrought imaginations of a husband who imagined the unfaithfulness of his wife— one who he fixedly ignores until it otherwise suits him."

Porthos took this opportunity to further needle his young companion. "Am I hearing that perhaps there was a reason for this husband's jealousy?"

"The queen's behavior is beyond reproach in whatever she should choose to do," defended D'Artagnan. "And if she should choose to bestow her friendship on a young musketeer, would I not be ungracious to refuse such a magnanimous gesture?"

"Whether the friendship be completely innocent or no," advised Athos, "one should tread with the utmost caution in such matters or…"

"Or one might find oneself relegated to roaming the Italian mountains with too small a saddle and wasting away on poorly cooked military fare," suggested Porthos, who had been complaining earlier that day that his waistline had been diminishing and that if better nourishment were not discovered he might soon be half the man.

D'Artagnan scowled. "Now that I have firmly felt the blame of our current predicament laid upon my shoulders—and am by Porthos's account single-handedly responsible for diminishing his great size and formidable strength—perhaps, Athos, you might continue to explain just why French troops are moving into Italy in the first place. Unless, perhaps, you feel this invasion of Italy is merely a pretext for King Louis to banish his own humble servant, myself, from court—but I do not feel I am of such importance to warrant a violation of another country's borders."

"Ah, do not underestimate yourself," replied Aramis. "Each one of us is of the greatest importance in God's eyes, and who is more god-like on Earth than the noble King Louis himself? In his pique he might move both Heaven and Earth to rid himself of a rival for the queen's affections—even if he only takes notice of her once or twice a year."

"How any man, be he king or musketeer, could fail to take notice of such a woman, I cannot understand," ruminated Porthos. "She rivals even

Madame Coquenard in her proportions and perhaps, though it may be indelicate for me to admit such a thing, she is even fairer of feature."

Madame Coquenard, the other musketeers knew, was Porthos's mysterious patron, who kept him in fine clothing and noble regalia. She was also the wife of a wealthy attorney and so Porthos did not often speak her name when inside the borders of France, lest rumor leak to her husband's ear that she was another man's mistress.

"None who has seen her can dispute the pleasant proportions of Madame Coquenard," replied Aramis. Though he was more overtly religious than the other musketeers, he was not immune to the attractions of the fairer sex. "But still, we have not settled the matter of why France enters Italy."

"I, for one, do not care," said Porthos. "As long as I find here the blood of enemies to slake my blade, wine to quench my thirst, and food to fill my belly, I shall be content." He shifted uncomfortably. "And perhaps I shouldn't forget to add that I might like to have my saddle returned by that most ungracious Captain Montagne."

"It is a simple matter, really," replied Athos, "though it is complicated by much genealogy, into which we shall not delve too deeply lest we confuse the basic issues."

"And what are the basic issues?" questioned D'Artagnan, who was most curious to find out for what cause he might soon be dying—setting aside his most reckless flirtations with Her Majesty, Queen Anne of Austria.

"Three men had direct claim to the duchies of Mantua and Monferrato," explained Athos.

"And one of those is clearly the Duke of Nevers who is a friend of France," finished Porthos, who was sure he had just satisfactorily comprehended the entirety of the situation in a matter of moments.

"No," replied Athos. "That would have simplified matters enormously, and if such were the case we would not likely be going to war with Spain."

"Then one or more of these three men have sided with Spain and are attempting to take back what is rightfully theirs from the Duke of Nevers?" suggested D'Artagnan.

"Alas," corrected Athos, "The three dukes of Mantua have all died: Francesco IV, Ferdinando, and Vincenzo II—brothers all of them."

"And what of their sons?" asked Porthos.

"Or of their daughters?" added Aramis, for he knew there was some precedent in Italy for royal lines passing through the women if there were no male heirs.

"They left nothing behind but bastard sons who hadn't been legitimized by their fathers and one daughter," replied Athos. "And so this left Mantua and Monferrato available to any enterprising distant relative in the Gonzaga Family line."

"I should like to be a duke one day," mused Porthos. "Perhaps I am distantly related to the Gonzaga Family."

"That is precisely the thinking that puts Mantua and Monferrato in their current predicament," said Athos.

"And just how distant is the Duke of Nevers from the the Dukes Francesco, Ferdinando, and Vincenzo?" asked D'Artagnan.

"Merely five degrees of consanguinity away," replied Athos. "And he cemented his claim by having his son Carlo marry Maria, the daughter of Duke Vincenzo."

"Ah hah," exclaimed Porthos. "So the Duke of Nevers has a clear claim to the duchies!"

"Not so clear that the Duke of Guastalla isn't contesting the claim," said Athos.

"And is he a closer relation to the ducal Gonzaga line?" questioned Aramis.

"He is six degrees of consanguinity away from the deceased dukes," replied Athos.

"And how does an Italian duke come to bring a Spanish army against an Italian fortress?" questioned D'Artagnan.

"The King of Spain is roused to action by the merest whiff of French involvement," said Athos. "Spain fears growing French influence in Italy, just as King Louis or, more accurately, Cardinale Richelieu fears growing Spanish influence in Italy. Because the Duke of Nevers has lands in France's Piedmont-Savoy, Spain perceives he has ties to the French and, indeed, the Duke of Nevers has manned his fortress with good French men drawn from those lands."

"So the Spanish flock to Casale Monferrato like maggots to a dead dog festering in the streets," said Porthos, waxing morbidly poetical.

"Well put, mon ami," said Athos. "But the Spanish may not be our only problem. The Duke of Guastalla also is friends with the Hapsburg Royalty of Austria."

"Spanish blood or Hapsburg blood," said Porthos with a shrug. "My sword doesn't care which it spills."

D'Artagnan's keen eyes viewed the forces that cordoned the fortress of Casale Monferrato. "I see plenty of Spanish banners, but no Hapsburg pennants."

"It is well," said Athos. "That means the Duke of Guastalla has not yet persuaded them to action."

"Let us make haste," urged Porthos. "This saddle made for babies is causing my behind to itch. I should like to break Duke Guastalla's forces and make it to the wall even before Captain Montagne has a chance to set his artillery emplacements."

"Agreed," said D'Artagnan. "That way he can make no claim that it was his cannonballs that frightened away the Spanish."

"The bulk of our troops are following the cannons, though," pointed out Aramis, who fingered his golden cross. "It will be some time before they are arrayed and ready for a charge."

"We will lose the element of surprise if we wait for them," said D'Artagnan.

"What need have we for troops?" questioned Porthos, voice bellowing with braggadocio. "Are we not the king's musketeers? And are there not four of us? Is that not enough to break any enemy line?"

"Then let us make haste!" Athos checked his brace of pistols and then the musket at the side of his horse.

When they were satisfied their firearms were securely loaded, they urged their horses down the mountain trail. Behind them, Captain Montagne swore at his gunners, urging them to greater speed as they dug emplacements for the cannons.

Still, he did not seem overly worried that the musketeers might reach the walls of the fortress, for he did not imagine they would be so reckless to approach the Spanish armies without the full strength of the French forces at their back. And even if he had conceived they might embark on such a foolhardy venture, he would have been even less concerned, for he would have imagined them being cut down by the thousand Spanish soldiers that ringed the fortress.

Likewise, Don Gonzalo Fernandez de Cordoba, the governor of Milan, who unfortunately controlled territories between the distant duchies of Mantua and Monferrato, had spotted the oncoming French forces but imagining they would take some time to form up and become a threat, quite leisurely commanded his forces to adjust to the new danger.

While flanking troops adjusted their positions, abandoning their fortifications around the fortress, the four musketeers unexpectedly galloped out of the foothills. At first, the Spanish armies did not know what to make of this quartet of riders. Since there were only four riders, they presumed the horsemen could not possibly be a part of the French forces who, they naturally figured, would attack en masse and with the support of artillery from the high ground. So the Spanish held their fire, figuring these were their own outriders who had been scouting the hills and were coming to report on the positions of the enemy French.

It was only when the riders were nearly upon them that they saw the colors of the blue and white and realized, to their great dismay and perplexion, that these riders were French musketeers. Then the musketeers were among them, slashing down any who came within reach of their swords and trampling those who were too slow to cast themselves away from the dashing hooves of their warhorses.

Don Gonzalo Fernandez de Cordoba was as surprised as any of his soldiers at this unlikely attack, but unsheathed his sword as the burliest of the musketeers barreled toward him on horseback. He was a fraction too slow and, though Porthos was busy hacking down a Spanish soldier on the other side of his mount; he managed to lift a great booted foot and plant it directly in Cordoba's chest, casting the Governor of Milan ten feet into the dirt and cracking a pair of his ribs in the process.

Porthos laughed uproariously at seeing a man of such high station cast down so ignominiously, but his mirth was drowned out by the thunder of D'Artagnan's pistols, as the young Gascon fired at Spanish soldiers who lowered their muskets to shoot the invading musketeers.

Aramis and Athos cut through the loosely gathered troops, carving away toward the walls of the fortress. So surprised were the Spanish forces by this unlikely assault that for a moment it appeared the four musketeers might actually reach the fortress, but once the troops recovered their senses a few of them began to fire at the French attackers.

Muskets cracked and a pair of lead balls whipped by Aramis's head. He silently thanked God for sending those missiles past him, plucked out a pistol from his belt, leaned back in his saddle, and fired at a Spanish musket man who was shooting at him from behind. Aramis's shot caught the Spanish soldier in the head, sending the doomed man reeling to the earth.

Athos deflected a sword blow and slashed open the face of a Spanish soldier, and then he was past the screaming man and into the open, only a hundred yards away from the bullet-pocked and cannon-battered stone walls of the fortress.

The French soldiers upon the wall had been watching this curious tableau with rapt interest, and they sent up a wild cheer as they saw Athos cut his way clear of the Spanish troops and break into the no man's land that was inhabited only by the strewn bodies of dead Spanish soldiers who had attempted to assault and break the high walls of the fortress. This land was cratered and soaked with blood, and a stench rose from the festering dead. Murders of crows, aroused by Athos's passing rose in bilious black clouds, shrieking out their displeasure at having their grisly meal disrupted.

In fact, it was only these ghastly carrion birds that saved the lives of Athos and Aramis who plunged into the swirling avian cacophony. For the murders of crows were so thick that the Spanish gunmen could no longer see the pair of musketeers, and they fired blindly into the cyclone of birds, adding further chaos to their frenzied flight.

D'Artagnan was about to break through the Spanish siege lines and brave the masses of crows and vultures, but a musket cracked as his horse leaped, a lead ball burying in the haunches of his steed, so that it shrieked out and fell.

Luckily, D'Artagnan managed to loose his feet from his stirrups and he was thrown shoulder over shank into the midst of the winged and wheeling avians. Stunned, he still managed to reel to his feet, but amidst the flapping wings and shrieking cries he could not see the Spanish siege lines nor the walls of Casale Monferrato.

In this confused state he decided on a direction and managed three faltering steps before he saw a great mass of horse and rider plunging through the whirling wings of angry birds. This rider, who was so prodigious, and who required a prodigious horse to carry him, leaned down and caught up D'Artagnan by the collar. There was such strength in that arm and shoulder, that the rider—who D'Artagnan suddenly recognized as the titanic Porthos—hoisted him bodily into the air and dropped him on the back of his horse.

"You were going the wrong way, my little friend!" quoth Porthos, who seemed somewhat jolly of temperament now that his sword had tasted blood and bullets had begun to fly thick in the air.

D'Artagnan was still confused. "But we are heading directly back into the Spanish lines!" he protested.

"Nonsense," cried Porthos. "You must have taken a knock on your skull. We are headed precisely in the direction of the fortress wall."

"But Athos and Aramis…"

"They are ahead of us," chided Porthos. "You shall see them momentarily!"

Indeed, the wheeling black kites, broad-winged vultures, and screaming crows cleared from their vision, revealing the scarred wall of the fortress looming so close that Porthos was forced to bring his horse to a rapid halt, causing it to rear up on its hind legs.

Only by catching onto Porthos's harness was D'Artagnan able to arrest his slide off the back of the horse. He heard shouts of admonition from above and he saw that the French soldiers atop the wall were throwing down rope lines from between the crenels of the ancient fortification and urging them to climb. In fact, D'Artagnan could see that Aramis and Athos had already abandoned their horses and were making impossibly swift time up the steep stone walls.

They ascended so rapidly that D'Artagnan thought they must be part lizard or gecko to accomplish such a feat, but then he realized the French soldiers were drawing up his companions as they climbed, which accounted for their too swift ascent.

"Go!" Porthos urged on D'Artagnan while drawing his pistols and firing at a pair of brave Spanish soldiers who had decided to dare the no-man's land in pursuit of the musketeers. These both fell dying to the blood-stained soil and immediately crows carpeted their bodies, pecking and plucking at the still thrashing Spanish men.

D'Artagnan stood on the back of Porthos's horse, caught an unrolling rope line and leapt upward. He fairly seemed to sprint up the wall as he was hoisted by a half dozen men. Lead balls spattered around him, but the birds were still thick in the air and no shot found D'Artagnan's flesh. In mere moments he had climbed the thirty foot wall and tumbled through the crenel, where French soldiers patted him on the shoulders and back, laughing and congratulating him on his foolhardy plunge through the Spanish ranks and out the other side to the relative security of the fortress Casale Monferrato.

Among the soldiers who had pulled him to safety, D'Artagnan caught sight an olive-skinned beauty with large dark eyes, and a wealth of black hair that spilled from beneath a blue beret. She was attired not in a gown or dress that might have befitted her extraordinary beauty, but rather blood-stained white trousers and a blue jacket of the French military.

This brief glance created a great impression, but then her face was lost amidst the sea of male soldiers who took hold of the other rope which they had thrown down to Porthos. When Porthos climbed from his too-small saddle and clamped his meaty hands around this rope, he nearly dragged six French soldiers through the crenels, for they had not accounted for his spectacular weight. Surely, any who laid their eyes upon this most doughty of musketeers would understand he was a big man, but beneath those layers of padded flesh lay heavy stripes of muscle which were nourished by a constant diet of raisins, nuts, dates, roasted chicken, beef, mutton, and downed

Lead balls spattered around him...

with liberal doses of honey and wine.

D'Artagnan saved this unsuspecting knot of men from being dragged to their doom, by grabbing hold of the rope and adding his wiry strength to that of the mob. He suddenly found himself shoulder to shoulder with the woman he had spotted moments before, and together they leaned back, adding their weight, so that the prodigious mass of Porthos could be momentarily suspended.

Still, gravity could not easily be defeated and it took twenty men to draw up the redoubtable form of Porthos, who was perspiring greatly by the time he reached the top of the wall—even though he had done little more than cling to the rope while the others had drawn him up.

He heaped his saviors with great praises while he crouched behind the up-jutting tooth of a crenel. "Par bleu, I counted fifty musket shots that struck the walls while I climbed aloft! Not a one of them found my flesh, except for this one that shaved my eyebrow!"

Indeed, a stripe had been burned through his left eyebrow, leaving a shaved mark through it.

"That shot came near to putting out your eye," said Athos.

"You should give praise to God when you say your rosaries," recommended Aramis.

Porthos clapped Aramis upon the shoulder with such force that it nearly buckled the other musketeer's knees. "That, mon ami, is why there is a great advantage to traveling with such a holy man as yourself! You shall say the rosaries for me, and I recommend you say at least a hundred of them so that God knows I am thankful for his preservation this day."

Aramis scowled when he realized how a hundred rosaries had suddenly been added to his already time consuming daily devotions. "Perhaps it would be more beneficial if you said your own rosaries."

"Nonsense!" said Porthos. "I would not dream of depriving you of the blessings and holiness that you have made your consuming goal—a goal even higher than that of service to your King, if I do daresay such a thing."

"There can be no goal higher than service to God," replied Aramis, but as the words left his mouth he realized he had been duped.

"Exactly, and that is why you shall say my rosaries for me," concluded Porthos.

"I begin to think," said Aramis, "that the general sentiment that you are slow-witted does not take into account a certain natural cunning which you possess."

"Nice of you to say so," replied Porthos, who appeared to take no offense at the statement—but whether this generally oblivious demeanor was affected or real, Aramis was still deciding.

In the meantime, a number of Spanish troops decided this might be a good time to assault the walls of Monferrato, but the attack was not directed by Governor Don Gonzalo Fernandez de Cordoba and so it came in ragged, poorly unorganized waves which were quickly routed with gunfire from the walls. Adding to the general confusion, Captain Montagne began a bombardment from the foothills.

The first few shots of this bombardment were illy placed and did no harm, but then Montagne began to perfect his mathematical wizardry and bounced the balls through the Spanish ranks, taking off legs and heads.

If Governor Don Gonzalo Fernandez de Cordoba needed any further enticement to withdraw from the field of battle, the three hundred French troops massing in the hills, preparing to sweep down upon the Spanish once they had been softened by cannon fire, seemed to have been the fait accompli.

Though Don Gonzalo Fernandez de Cordoba had a thousand Spanish troops at his command, and might have still won the day if he were able to redirect some of his artillery toward the hills and mass half of his men against the oncoming French relief, his troops were in chaos due to the surprise rush of musketeers through their ranks. Additionally, the ill-advised and impromptu attack on the walls of the fortress which had been initiated by some of his lieutenants had caused some confusion among the troops.

Given that his ribs had nearly been stoved in by Porthos's mighty kick, the Governor Don Gonzalo Fernandez de Cordoba decided perhaps a strategic retreat might be in order, for he mistakenly feared that the three hundred French troops he saw massing in the hills might only be the forefront of French relief effort. Painfully crawling onto his horse, he gave the orders to fall back.

The Spanish retreat was disorderly and they left behind many tents and provisions, which the French troops were all too glad to loot and pillage once they moved onto the plains outside of the fortress.

Porthos leaned heavily on a cracking crenel, previously weakened by Spanish cannon shot, and with great satisfaction viewed the fleeing Spanish. "Look at the whipped dogs run, Athos! Is it not a pleasant and satisfactory sight?"

"It is indeed," said Athos, but with a hint of reservation in his voice.

Porthos did not fail to hear this hesitation. "What, do you not share my joy at seeing our enemies defeated and fleeing like lambs before a mighty lion?!"

"I do indeed," said Athos, "but they flee merely because their hearts faltered—not because we dealt them a devastating defeat. We killed perhaps two score men…"

"Yes!" exclaimed Porthos. "Two score Spanish dead and not a single French casualty—except for me perhaps. It shall be most embarrassing if we are recalled to the court of the king and I am missing an eyebrow."

Athos was amused at this vanity, but did not comment upon it.

"Anyhow, save my wounded pride, the French are the clear victors this day!" continued Porthos.

"We are indeed," said Athos, "but it is not a decisive enough victory to discourage the Spanish from coming at us again. I fear they shall be back and with greater numbers. King Louis did not see fit to send enough troops to defend against the Governor Don Gonzalo Fernandez de Cordoba if he should return with twice as many men."

"These are strong walls!" protested Porthos. "They can stand for years against the cannon fire of the Spanish." But even as he spoke, the crenel against which he leaned began to grind, a crack in its face growing larger, and suddenly the doughty musketeer found it was no longer supporting his weight.

He managed to regain his balance, but watched mournfully as the broken crenel tumbled down the wall, breaking into smaller pieces of rubble. "Perhaps my estimation of the strength of the fortress has been overly optimistic," Porthos conceded. "If it cannot stand the weight of one mere musketeer, perhaps it will not be able to stand against two thousand Spanish and their cannons."

In the meantime, D'Artagnan sought out the company of the olive-skinned woman in the blue beret with whom he had worked shoulder to shoulder in hoisting Porthos's immense bulk to the top of the ramparts. She peered between a gap in the crenels, a smoking musket in her hand and surveying the form of a wounded Spanish soldier who still groaned and heaved thirty yards from the wall.

"The poor fellow is wounded in the belly," observed D'Artagnan. "It might take him days to expire."

The dark-haired beauty turned and for a moment D'Artagnan thought he detected a gleam in her eye, but surely it was a trick of the sunlight or a figment of his imagination, because such delight in the suffering of another did not become a woman of such beauty. "I fear, monsieur, that it was my shot that put him in such a fatal condition—but I am afraid I do not know how to reload this musket and put the suffering man out of his misery. I cannot bear to see him linger long, tormented by his pain and in the hot sun."

"Perhaps, once Captain Montagne and his soldiers have finished looting they will find him and administer the coup de grace," suggested D'Artagnan.

"Perhaps," said the dark-haired woman, her beauty radiant despite the man's uniform she wore. "Please excuse my poor manners and unpresentable dress. When I saw the Spanish forces arrayed against Casale Monferrato I could not permit myself to remain inactive and in hiding with the women and children. So I disguised myself as a man in order to help defend the walls."

"A poor disguise," said D'Artagnan, "for even a man half blind could detect your feminine charms, despite the soldier's uniform. And what French soldier ever possessed such a glorious and lustrous mane of hair?"

She laughed with delight at D'Artagnan's compliment. "It was only necessary for me to fool the soldiers long enough to gain the wall. Once here, they were too worried about the Spanish to banish me from the wall—even though it was quickly discovered I was no man."

"I am D'Artagnan of Gascon, one of King Louis' four musketeers which he sent to the aid of the Casale Monferrato."

She rose and extended her gun-powder charred hand. "And I am the Countess Ludovica Bianchi. It is a pleasure to meet you."

"The Countess Bianchi?" repeated D'Artagnan with a gallant bow as he took her hand. "Never did I think to meet a Countess upon the battlements of Casale Monferrato."

"Surely," said the Countess Bianchi, "King Louis sent more than merely four musketeers to the aid of Casale Monferrato."

"Nay," said D'Artagnan.

"Then the King must hold you in high regard—must consider you the elite of the elite if he expects just four of you to turn the tide against the Spanish," flattered the Countess Bianchi.

"We were accompanied by three hundred soldiers and artillery," said D'Artagnan with uncharacteristic humility—a trait which neither he nor Porthos were unduly afflicted with. "It is not as if we alone caused the Spanish to turn tail and run!"

"I know not," said the Countess Bianchi coyly. "After all, your wild charge caused them much discomfiture and confusion they were not able to assemble their ranks before being assaulted by the second wave of French."

D'Artagnan was quite pleased by this assessment, but attempted not to glow with overmuch pride. "We merely did our duty, Countess."

"Well, I owe you much for your gallant charge—and if the people of Casale Monferrato do not repay the instrument of their salvation, I surely will."

While D'Artagnan's mind lingered on the infinite possibilities of this statement, The Countess Bianchi thrust the musket into the musketeer's hands.

"Perhaps you can see fit to do me another service, D'Artagnan of King Louis' musketeers. Reload this musket and finish the Spanish soldier below, before his groans wake the slain from the dust of the battlefield."

D'Artagnan complied by tilting the frizzen forward and opening the pan of the musket. He produced a paper cartridge from the pouch on his belt, ripped it open with his teeth, pulled the hammer back to cock, poured in a small amount of gunpowder from the cartridge and closed the frizzen to keep the priming powder trapped. He sifted the rest of the powder down the barrel, reversed the cartridge and pushed in the ball and then the wadding of the paper. In a moment he used a rod to ram it home. All this he accomplished with a practiced rapidity.

Resting the musket on the top of a crenel he sighted in on the dying Spanish soldier and fired. The musket bucked against his shoulder, and the Spanish soldier gave a final twitch and died.

"You are very merciful to think about the pain of a dying enemy," said D'Artagnan.

"When my husband died, he lingered for months of agony before finally the reaper claimed him one cold night," replied the Countess. "It is a horrible thing to see—even amongst the enemy."

With the fortress secure, the four musketeers eventually were able to venture outside and retrieve their horses—all except for D'Artagnan's whose unfortunate steed had met his demise charging through the Spanish gauntlet.

"No matter," said the Countess Bianchi as D'Artagnan mourned the loss of his horse. "My husband possessed a fine horse with a temperament well-suited for battle. Come to 66 Strada Centrale this evening to dine with me and I shall send you away with a horse worthy of a musketeer."

When the Countess Bianchi had departed, Athos looked upon D'Artagnan with a severe expression. "Scarcely do you escape trouble with one woman and you find trouble with another. Beware lest word of this come to the ears of the Queen and she be jealous. It would not be well for you to incur the wrath of both the King and the Queen. If the Queen should be angered with you, who will protect you from the King?"

D'Artagnan, not tempered by the wisdom of age and experience, and still full of the indiscretion of youth gave a dismissive smile. "You worry overmuch, Athos. The Countess Bianchi merely wants to gift me with an unused horse so I am equally mounted with my estimable brothers-in-arms—and as for Queen Anne, she will not hear of any dalliance that takes place so many leagues away."

"Perhaps that last is true or perhaps not," said Athos, who was the wisest of the musketeers—much of this learned by hard and painful experience, which made him often melancholy. "But I do not think the Countess Bianchi's designs stop at gifting you merely with a horse."

"I won't be in Casale Monferrato long enough to create any lasting attachments of the heart," protested D'Artagnan. "Soon King Louis will forget his jealousy and call us back to defend him in his palace—or perhaps to put down some isolated pocket of Huguenots which has risen up once more in rebellion."

"Take a care," warned Athos again, though he feared his cautions would go unheeded. "Words travel far and quickly—sometimes as if on the wind or on the wings of a bird. How will it seem to the Queen if she hears her favorite at court has so quickly succumbed to the charms of a widowed Italian Countess? There is no wrath like a woman and especially a queen who has been cast aside for another."

"I shall take your words under advisement," replied D'Artagnan, "but, to my great regret, I am sure the Countess Bianchi has no romantic designs upon me. Is she not quite lovely to look upon—even in a blood-soiled uniform meant to be worn by a man?"

"She is quite a different woman than the one who first married the Count Bianchi. She has changed much since her husband's death," interrupted a short and well-dressed Italian man who introduced himself as Pierro Ricci, erstwhile governor of Casale Monferrato. He profusely thanked them and the absent King Louis for their timely intervention.

Before any further speculations upon romance or lovely women could be undertaken, Porthos posed a question. "And where is the Duke of Nevers who is the ruler of this Duchy? Shouldn't he be here defending his lands?"

"The Duke of Nevers suffers from the challenge of ruling two duch-ies who are separated by Italian and French controlled lands," replied Governor Ricci. "The Duke, unfortunately, cannot be in two places at once. Upon hearing about the siege of Casale Monferrato he raised soldiers and took them against towns surrounding Milan, hoping to cause the Duke of Guastalla to call back Don Gonzala Fernandez de Cordoba. However, that gambit, I fear, was a failure. If you had not arrived we should still be under siege."

"Why does not the Duke of Nevers just consolidate his holdings by taking everything between Mantua and Monferrato?" questioned Porthos, who viewed all problems simple and complex with equally broad responses.

"He does not have enough soldiers for such an undertaking," replied Governor Ricci, "and the politics here are very complicated. There is a delicate balance between French, Spanish, and Italian influence. Even the mere act of claiming the Gonzaga birthright over Mantua and Monferrato upset the apple cart, I am afraid."

"Then right the apple cart!" proclaimed Porthos. "How hard can it be to pick up a few loose fruits? If I were not the king's musketeer, I might deign accomplish the task myself—and I might eat a few of these apples to fill my empty belly."

Governor Ricci furrowed his brow, not sure whether Porthos was purposely obfuscating the conversation or merely did not understand his analogy. "Perhaps I have misspoken in comparing our dire situation to fruit. However, I am very grateful for the aid you have provided. Now that the Spanish have seen we are backed by the might of the French, perhaps they will think twice about coming against us."

All the talk of apples had caused Porthos's belly to begin rumbling. He rubbed ruefully at the cavernous space. "I'm afraid our engagement with the enemy has caused me to work up an appetite."

"Is there anything," replied Aramis, "that does not cause you to work up an appetite, my dear friend?"

Porthos considered this and shook his impressively maned head. "The mere act of waking up in the morning causes my belly to rumble—so I must agree that almost anything causes hunger."

"Please dine with me in the Governor's mansion," invited Governor Ricci. "I have stables with plenty of hay and room for your horses."

They proceeded through the fortress of Monferrato Casale which encompassed much of the town. Signs of deprivations were showing wherever they looked: the men, women, and children thin of limb and shrunken of belly. Already, they were gathering foraging parties to go outside of the walls of the fortress to search for food.

"I have already sent a messenger to Duke Nevers in Mantua to have them send provisions," said Governor Ricci. "We have been unable to restock our supplies since the siege sequestered us from outside trade."

They passed a high-steepled church with stained glass windows. The lower windows and the doors had all been nailed over.

"Why is the church boarded shut?" questioned Aramis, whose delicate religious sensibilities were offended at such a sight. "At a time of such exigency that war brings, certainly the citizens of Casale Monferrato have more need for religion than at any other time!"

"It grieves my soul as well," replied Governor Ricci. "But I am afraid the clergy of Casale Monferrato has come to untimely end via illness."

"All of them?" questioned an astounded Aramis.

"Not all," said Governor Ricci, "but those who did not succumb to the illness—which resembled the plague—fled the city. And just in time, I might add, for they managed to depart prior to arrival of Don Gonzala Fernandez de Cordoba and his troops."

"Do you think they knew of the impending siege?" questioned Athos shrewdly.

"I have no indication they did," replied Governor Ricci, "but they were certainly frightened of something—though at the time I thought it was the illness that had wrought fear in them."

"Was there any other sign of plague in Casale Monferrato?" questioned Aramis.

"None," admitted Governor Ricci. "The illness was confined solely to the clergy. It was a curious thing, but I had no answers for it. Who but God Himself can explain such mysteries?"

"Indeed," replied Aramis, in complete agreement. "Though I would be curious to understand the mysteries of God's mind from time to time."

"It surprises me to hear a man of God such as yourself speak such heresy," said Athos. "I am not offended, but certainly there are priests and cardinals who would find such words blasphemous and say it is not for man to know the mysteries of God."

"Perhaps," admitted Aramis. "But does not God occasionally deign to reveal a fraction of his mysteries to his people, the same as if a shaft of sunlight pierces a stormy sky and falls upon one object, illuminating it in golden brilliance! Did not God write the Ten Commandments in the stone tablets atop of Mount Sinai? Did he not part the Red Seas and open the way of the Israelites to inherit the promised land?"

"All indisputable," replied Athos.

All this talk of religion and God was making Porthos sleepy. "Good Governor, you shouldn't happen to have a place where four poor musketeers can lay their heads? Perhaps in the stalls alongside our horses?"

"I won't hear of such a thing!" exclaimed Governor Ricci. "I have extra rooms and soft beds should you do me the honor of staying this evening."

"A soft bed," repeated Porthos. "That would indeed be a tonic for my bruised backside!"

"Then it is settled," Athos told Governor Ricci. "We should be very grateful for your hospitality."

That hospitality, as it turned out stretched from one night into three months. Though D'Artagnan spend very few of them in his quarters, instead disappearing into the Countess's abode at 66 Strada Centrale. The platonic gift of horse and trappings it seemed came with other more personal gifts, which kept D'Artagnan occupied for many of his evenings. The Countess proved to be a very diverting companion with the curious habit of disappearing for a few minutes—as the bustle of the servants died away—each time before they retired to her chambers. Usually, she visited the galley, then disappeared into the cellar, reappearing with a bottle of wine of some obscure vintage.

The Spanish did not return after their initial route, but Governor Ricci weekly received reports of activity. Still, despite the rumors, neither Duke Guastalla nor Don Gonzalo Fernandez de Cordoba made an appearance in the following three months. Aramis spent much of this time improving upon the fortifications of Casale Monferrato, supervising the construction of additional defensive structures and buttressing walls damaged in the siege.

Athos, although allowing Aramis to take the lead on such matters, occasionally interjected a thought or two on the defenses, the wisdom of which became immediately apparent upon reflection. This saved weeks of wasted effort and resulted in a more formidable fortress that transformed formerly weak points into points of strength.

"Funnel the enemy into this channel, where the wall was formerly nigh on collapse," suggested Athos. "Then they will be caught between the grape shot of these cannons."

Governor Ricci enthusiastically embraced the guidance of the musketeers, and Porthos and D'Artagnan made themselves useful by drilling the French and Italian troops in their musketry until soon each of the troops were able to reload their muskets in less than thirty seconds.

"What of sword training?" questioned one Italian soldier.

"If we train you well enough with the musket," replied D'Artagnan, "you'll kill the Spanish before they ever reach the walls of Fortress Monferrato.

"Once your skill with the musket has been perfected, then we will address the art of swordplay," added Porthos. "I shall personally teach you how to dice the enemy into mincemeat!"

As it turned out, this was never to be. A message arrived from the Court of France with the seal of King Louis, and Governor Ricci personally read it to them in his office, so that no other ears might hear the words of the king, lest there be something confidential held within.

"Seeing that our French troops have successfully driven off the Spanish, Captain Montagne and his artillery, his troops and the musketeers Athos, Aramis, and Porthos are recalled to Paris to continue to serve at the pleasure and will of King Louis the 8th."

D'Artagnan bolted from his seat at this. "What of me? Am I not mentioned in the order?!"

Governor Ricci ran his finger down the lines of the letter. "Indeed, you are mentioned in the next paragraph." He continued to read from the royal missive. "The musketeer D'Artagnan will continue indefinitely at Casale Monferrato to train the troops of the Duke of Nevers, serving under his direction, until such time I decree his service has been sufficient."

D'Artagnan sank into his seat and put his hand to his head. "Woe is mine. I am to be separated from my brothers and forever lost from memory in the depths of Italia!"

"Do not lose hope," replied Aramis. "We will gauge the climate of the court once we return and speak highly of your exploits here so that you are not forgotten. And, when the moment is amenable, we will speak in the right ears so that you might be recalled."

"I know it is of small consolation," spoke the diminutive Governor of Casale Monferrato, "but I shall be pleased to have your continued services. I am not so confident as King Louis that our troubles with the Duke of Guastalla are finished."

"Perhaps with further drilling your men can fire thrice in a minute," considered D'Artagnan. "That would put up a fearsome volley that any Spaniard would hesitate to throw themselves into."

"That's the spirit!" Athos clapped D'Artagnan on the shoulder. "You shall make the best of your exile—just as we have all done while we are here."

"Casale Monferrato is a fine place," protested Governor Ricci. "The air is good, the climate temperate, and the women beautiful. I do not understand why you should all be so anxious to leave my company."

"It is all the things you say it is," agreed Aramis, "but it is not France—and there is no other city like Paris in the world with its tall cathedrals and collection of holy relics."

"You shall make the best of your exile..."

Porthos nudged D'Artagnan. "There is at least one beautiful woman who will not be sad to find out you will be staying a mite longer."

"Do you think the queen has learned of my affair with the Countess?" asked D'Artagnan. "And that perhaps she is behind my continued stay in Casale Monferrato?"

"That we shall not know until we reach court," said Athos, "and even so it may take us some time to learn just what the queen knows or just what she does not know. This might simply be a case of King Louis still being angered by the attentions the queen was bestowing upon you."

"Either one is bad enough," said Porthos, without tact. "If the king becomes too jealous he just might give the word to have you guillotined—and if the queen becomes too jealous, she might just as easily persuade the king to order you guillotined."

"Considering the options," said Aramis, "An extended stay in Casale Monferrato may the best for your health."

"It is a salutary environment," agreed Governor Ricci. "Though too many have chosen to depart us of late."

"No wonder, if they caught wind of a Spanish invasion!" burst out Porthos in his often exuberant manner.

"Perhaps so," replied Governor Ricci, "but we had little warning."

The attentions of the Countess Bianchi were a fine consolation for his separation from his friends, admitted D'Artagnan to himself as he recalled the curving lines of her figure, her deep red lips drawn back from pearly teeth, and the passionate embraces which they shared. That night, after his fellow musketeers had departed for France, he found himself again entwined in the Countess's arms and she kissed his forlorn mood away, so that it dissolved into fevered ardor.

"You are a musketeer, whatever land you should find yourself in," she murmured in his ear. "It does not matter if you are in France, Italy, or if you should find yourself in the savage lands across the oceans. You should spend every night with me and I will make you forget Paris and Queen Anne."

"Queen Anne?" questioned D'Artagnan. "How do you know of her?"

"You speak in your sleep, my dearest D'Artagnan. Now tell me truth, have you ever felt such passions in the embrace of even the Queen of France as you have felt in my arms?"

"Never have I embraced the Queen of France," admitted D'Artagnan.

"Hah, so it is unrequited love—or at least unconsummated love," said the Countess Bianchi. "What kind of romance can there be in a situation where a woman belongs to another? Me, I am unencumbered by husband and free to bestow my entire affections on who I choose—and I choose you, my young Gascon! If you chose to marry me, that would make you the Count Bianchi and you would inherit the noble title and properties of my dearly departed."

"What happened to your husband?" questioned D'Artagnan.

"He was three decades older than me," said the Countess. "It was a political marriage made to strengthen the position of my family, which had fallen from favor and wealth. Anyhow, my husband died while climbing the stairs one sweltering afternoon. His heart failed and he broke his neck while tumbling backward."

D'Artagnan had himself been up the steep and winding stairs of the household many times to visit the Countess Bianchi's chambers. "He died on the very stairs of this house?"

"Not the stairs of this house, but on the stairs of the crypt beneath the church."

"The boarded church? What was he doing in the crypt?"

"No one knows—least of all me," said the Countess. "He was a very secretive and cruel man. And truth be told, I was not sad at his demise—though I wore black and went through my dutiful period of mourning."

That night, D'Artagnan was still restless and slept fitfully. Long after the Countess had lapsed into slumber, he heard a tapping noise which he at first ignored. When it persisted, he rose, donned his trousers and went to the balcony. The warm wind blew against his bare chest and ruffled his hair, but the streets of Casale Monferrato were empty, the ruddy moon revealing no nocturnal adventurers wandering the city.

D'Artagnan returned into the manse, and briefly surveyed the magnificent figure of the Countess Bianchi swathed in the linens of the bed. She rolled onto her side without rousing from her slumber. Still, the rhythmic tapping continued and so the musketeer plucked up his sword from where it hung upon the bedpost, fired a lantern, and wandered the narrow halls of the Bianchi manse, head cocked so he might ascertain the direction of the mysterious clicking noise that had roused him from his sporadic sleep.

The servants of the manse were nowhere to be seen, having long ago retired to their own chambers. D'Artagnan pursued the sound down those precipitous and winding stairs which he had falsely feared might have been the cause of the Count Bianchi's demise, and then down another flight of stairs into a cellar well-stocked with preserves and the fantastic array of wines of which he and the Countess Bianchi had nightly been availing themselves.

Past these rows of dusty bottles, D'Artagnan followed the noise until he came to a stone wall from behind which he swore he could hear the insistent tapping. He lifted the lantern to examine the seeping stones and found there was a seam that rose from the floor to about the height of his waist, crossed two feet and descended again to the floor.

After close examination found the floorboards of the cellar had been disturbed. Setting his lantern on the floor, he managed to pry up a loosened board. This revealed a catch, which he loosed and then he hauled upward on a pair of leather straps, so that a small section of the wall slid upward and rotated outward.

In this instant the light of his lantern revealed an unfathomable sight that caused D'Artagnan to reel backward in shock and incomprehension. For there, crouched in a cramped and cell-like cubicle, bound hand and foot, and gagged with a strip of cloth between her teeth, was the Countess Bianchi who he had left asleep in her chambers above!

Though her hands were bound behind her back, she clutched a small stone with which she had been tapping against the wall of her prison, and this miniscule noise—in the dead of night—had carried through the stone walls of the manse to D'Artagnan's ears.

When finally D'Artagnan overcame his initial shock, though his bewilderment had not in the least abated, he drew his sword and used the tip to sever the woman's bonds, then he helped her out of her cramped cell and into the cellar. He rested his sword against a wine rack and unknotted the gag, noting that the clothing the Countess wore did not at all resemble the clothing she had shed before climbing into bed with D'Artagnan earlier than night.

In fact, she wore a ragged dressing gown that did not in the least resemble any that D'Artagnan had seen in the Countess's collection. All these thoughts came swiftly, in a jumbled wave, without his mind being able to sort or fathom any underlying meaning or reason.

"What are you doing down here, Countess?!" exclaimed D'Artagnan. "I left you in bed minutes ago…"

The answer was cold and not without a hint of bitterness. "You did not leave me in bed, stranger. You left my sister, Martina, in my bed. I am the Countess Ludovica Bianchi."

D'Artagnan faltered. "I don't understand."

"Of course, you don't," replied the woman who claimed to be the Countess Ludovica Bianchi. "My sister is a very clever woman and, unfortunately, looks exactly like me, save for a birthmark I do not possess—one on her belly in the shape of a club. I presume you're familiar with it?"

Indeed, D'Artagnan had taken notice of this peculiar marking—but he thought it might be an impropriety to admit this—even though he had already inadvertently revealed his entire affair to this prisoner while he was laboring under the apparently mistaken impression that she was the same woman as her sister. "So why are you kept prisoner in the cellar?"

This question did not immediately get answered. "Are you sure that Martina still sleeps?"

"She was sound asleep when I heard you tapping and left the room," said D'Artagnan, who was still grappling for some sort of meaning behind this strange turn of events.

"Perhaps she was merely pretending!" Ludovica laid her hand upon D'Artagnan's arm. "You must take me away from here before Martina discovers I have been let out of my cell!"

D'Artagnan wasn't sure of much except that he couldn't allow this lovely creature to be forced back into the tiny cell in which she had been imprisoned. But the woman he had left in her chambers upstairs possessed precisely the same loveliness, and he couldn't imagine her capable of locking her own sister into a cell and depriving her of light and comfort. Still, hadn't he seen hints of cruelty in occasional unguarded comments and a hint of delight in her expression when she had heard the tortured cries of the dying Spanish man she had shot from the walls of Casale Monferrato? Is it possible that the woman who he had been having a three month love affair with was a monster along the lines of the Milady DeWinter whose snares he had once fallen into?

Ludovica could sense the musketeer's hesitation. "My husband has an armoire of clothing on the main level. You could wear his shirt and boots and take me somewhere else."

"I have a room at Governor Ricci's home," said D'Artagnan. "Do you know where it is?"

"I know where it is, but it is better if you take me," replied Ludovica. "The streets of Casale Monferrato are no longer safe for a lone woman at night and it would be better, for the nonce, if no one knows where I am. For if a servant with loose lips should speak that the Countess Bianchi came to the home of Governor Ricci, that rumor might come back to the ears of my sister. She should know where to find me and send her cult members after me so that I might be imprisoned again and sacrificed to the plague god Resheph!"

"Resheph?" questioned D'Artagnan.

"His very name translates into burning fever, plague and pestilence!" exclaimed Ludovica. "It is found on the tablets discovered in the ruins of Ebla. He is one of the gods of the four gates of Ebla!"

D'Artagnan retrieved his sword and handed his lantern to the woman who claimed to be the Countess Ludovica Bianchi. "And where is this Ebla you speak of?"

"In Syria—for Resheph is a god of the deserts, and his power is derived from the dry wastes and the wet blood of innocents."

D'Artagnan, having decided to at least usher this woman to the safety of his apartments in the manse of Governor Ricci, led the way up the steep stairs from the cellar. "And how does an Italian Countess know so much about heathen deities from the Eastern countries?"

"My husband—the Count Bianchi—was a perverse man who turned his back on Christ long before I ever married him. He took pleasure in the pagan and sensual rites of the strange gods—and Resheph in particular."

They crept into the shadowed halls and corridors of the mansion's main floor, and now Ludovica took the lead, her bare feet padding across the tiled floors, the frayed hem of her tattered night dress trailing, and her long black hair falling in matted tangles around her shoulders.

"None of this explains how your sister ended up the Countess Bianchi and you a prisoner in your own home," protested D'Artagnan.

She opened up an armoire situated in the back hall and sighed with relief when she saw it was still filled with an assortment of male and female clothing. "My sister hasn't yet thrown away my husband's clothing—probably so her lovers have convenient clothing to wear."

"Attend!" replied D'Artagnan. "Lovers? You mean there are others besides me?"

Ludovica looked askance at the young musketeer. "Perhaps none so young and handsome, but did you imagine that you were her only lover since my husband died? My sister has an insatiable appetite and has entertained a string of men who she tires of and discards—if they are fortunate. For if they begin to comprehend who she really is, she arranges for them to disappear via accident or to be called away to some other town on the prospect of business or urgent family matters."

Strangely, D'Artagnan's pride was wounded by this revelation of multiple lovers, more than he was concerned about the disappearance of them. "And just how many of these have there been?"

"It has been difficult for me to keep track of them. I hear different voices enter the household and then, before entertaining them, my sister brings me a drugged porridge which supplies both nourishment and the merciful oblivion of sleep.

"And tonight," said D'Artagnan. "She forgot to excuse herself before we—"

"Yes," said Ludovica. "She left me awake to tap at the wall. The only way I could find to communicate with you."

D'Artagnan set aside his sword and pulled on the over large chemise, a hideous thing lined with double rows of ostentatious brass buttons each the size of a franc, which Ludovica had proffered him. Then he sat on a bench and pulled on a pair of too small shoes. "What of the servants? Are they not aware you have been kept prisoner by your sister? Surely they would have helped you!"

"The servants are told a wild animal is being kept! None of them have ever looked upon me, and they are told to ignore whatever noises they hear."

"Then they shall not be awakened as we pilfer the closets," suggested D'Artagnan.

"We are not pilfering them," Ludovica reminded the musketeer. "This entire manse and everything in it belongs to me."

"Then why not awaken the servants and command them to throw your sister into the streets?" suggested D'Artagnan, but his heart was wounded by his own words even as he said them, for though the evidence was before his own eyes, he could not imagine his lover was cruel enough to imprison her own sister. To suggest that his lover be thrown into the streets seemed an inexcusable gratitude for all the pleasure he had received by her.

"And don't you think the servants would be just as confused as you are?" asked Ludovica. "They will see twin sisters with no discernible difference except for the deplorable state of my grooming. Which one of us would they believe? You believe me not because you detect any inherent honesty in my voice, but only because you found me bound and gagged in the prison of my sister's making."

"I hope I have not offended you by showing any doubt to the veracity of your words," said D'Artagnan. "It's just that your story is so wild that only the evidence of my own eyes causes me to believe it."

Ludovica selected a dress. "Turn your back while I change my attire."

"Naturally," said D'Artagnan, who turned, but in doing so caught a glimpse of Ludovica's reflection in the mirror inside the open door of the armoire. He saw an expanse of olive-tinted back which possessed the same lovely form as her sister, and then she ducked and pulled on her dress.

"Help me fasten the back," requested Ludovica.

There were still many gaps to the story Ludovica had told, and D'Artagnan was about to request more of the story when he caught sight of an accustomed figure in a flimsy dressing gown approaching from the corridor beyond Ludovica.

It was Martina and she was carrying one of D'Artagnan's muskets in each hand. At first, Ludovica did not see her, for she was distracted in trying to fasten her dress.

Martina extended both flintlock pistols, the hammers cocked back. She pointed one at the musketeer and the other at her erstwhile prisoner. "So, D'Artagnan, I see you have discovered my dirty little secret. It's too bad, because I wasn't yet tired of your company. Now, I shall have to dispose of you earlier than I anticipated."

D'Artagnan's jaw dropped open. "So, it is true! I didn't want to believe what this was woman was telling me—hoped there was some sort of explanation for your sordid behavior."

"You've taken great interest in my sordid behavior," teased Martina. "Help me lock my poor little sister back up and we may continue our nocturnal activities."

"I will not be a knowing party to imprisoning your own sister!" protested D'Artagnan.

"I am sorry to hear you say that, D'Artagnan. It appears, in that case, you shall soon be the unfortunate victim of your own pistol."

"The Governor shall come asking you questions if I disappear," warned D'Artagnan. "You shan't escape justice."

Martina gave a low chuckle. "I have so far. I see no reason, with the continued blessing of Resheph, that should not continue."

"So even the stories about the worship of some ludicrous demon plague god are truth." D'Artagnan edged an inch closer to his sword.

Martina's eyes burned with an angry fire. "Ludicrous, you say?! Do you think the clergy of Monferrato's parish all died from the happenstance of contracting a plague? I and the worshipers of Resheph cursed them with that same plague and defiled the crypts beneath for our own rites. With the sacrifice of my own flesh and blood, this very night, just before the dawn breaks we shall bring Resheph's curse down on all of Italy, and perhaps all of the world!"

"That is very interesting," said D'Artagnan, shifting just a bit closer to his sword, so it was nearly within reach.

"Don't patronize me." Martina fired one of her pistols, the flame lighting up the surrounding walls and the boom resounding in the confined space. Black gun smoke billowed into the air and D'Artagnan felt a bullet hammer into his chest. It knocked him down and he gasped for breath that wouldn't seem to come.

Martina leaned over the fallen musketeer and observed the spreading crimson stain over his heart. She laughed in delight when she saw his struggles to breath. "That's right, young Gascon. Struggle for life even as it inevitably slips away. I actually dismissed the servants from the manse last night before we retired. I'll be back after morning light to write your suicide note. It will be a poignant message about how you could not bear to be parted in disgrace from your fellow musketeers and confessing your secret love for the Queen. It will touch Queen Anne's heart to know that her love for you was enough to cause you take your own life."

These were the last words D'Artagnan heard before blackness closed in around the edges of his vision and then completely obscured him in its aphotic fog.

When D'Artagnan awoke, the pain in his chest let him know he was still in the land of the living. His lantern had burned to a dull glow that flickered across the tiles of the floor which were spattered with his own blood. He hoisted himself into a sitting position against the bench and probed the wound over his heart. He was surprised to find the bullet close to the surface, lodged in his flesh. With his fingers he pried it out, but when he examined it in the feeble light he was surprised to find it was no bullet at all, but rather one of the great brass buttons of the chemise which he had found so ostentatious. It had been pushed into the flesh by the impact of the bullet, which had been deflected, cutting a furrow across his chest as it ricocheted away.

It must have been the shock of the impact of the bullet over his heart which had caused him to lapse into unconsciousness. D'Artagnan bitterly remonstrated himself for having lapsed into such a useless condition after receiving what amounted to a flesh wound, but there was nothing that could be done for it now.

He searched his hazy memory for the events that had led up to his unconsciousness and managed to recall the last words of Martina, the false Countess Bianchi. So when he saw no sign of the actual Countess Ludovica Bianchi, he knew what he needed to do.

He discovered one of his pistols, the one with which he had been shot, lying in the nearby shadow, and his sword on the floor where he must have knocked it when he fell. These he reclaimed and, climbing to the upper floor of the manse, he recovered his cartridge pouch and boots. Once he had reloaded his pistol, he left the empty Bianchi Manse and headed for the church so long ago abandoned by the Catholic clergy for fear of the plague which had spread amongst them.

The great stain glass murals of the high tower seemed somehow sinister in the wan light of the falling moon. D'Artagnan made a covert investigation of the boarded entrances to the desolate cathedral and in a narrow alley behind he found muddy tracks on a trio of crates stacked like steps. These led to an empty window covered by propped planks that swung open on single nails. On the edge of the window frame he found a piece of torn cloth that resembled the same material from which Ludovica's replacement dress had been tailored.

This provided a confirmation that D'Artagnan's hunch had been correct, so he determined to continue in an effort to save Ludovica from the grim fate which her twin sister had promised. Traces of some fetid stench wafted out when he lifted the board but not seeing or hearing anything in the blackness beyond, he quickly scrambled through the casement and found himself in the somber chapel, moonlight trickling in a rainbow through high unboarded stained glass murals that depicted sword bearing angels treading demons beneath their hallowed feet.

If only, thought D'Artagnan, that were always the case—for it seemed far too often that on this sordid earth that the opposite occurred. But now he was thinking like Aramis, or perhaps he had merely been persuaded to Aramis's somber musings and religious philosophies which he often expounded upon late nights around dying campfires with the panoply of God's creation twinkling in the black of the firmament.

He wished now that he might have the firm resolution of Aramis's faith alongside him as he went to face the devil Resheph, not to mention Aramis's quick sword. Still, he breathed a prayer even while thinking himself unworthy to have it answered, considering his almost nightly lustful dalliances with the woman he had thought to be the Countess Bianchi.

As he crept from the chapel he found a row of votive candles glimmering and flickering in a noxious draft. D'Artagnan searched for the source of this draft and discovered an open hatch and a stair which descended into the crypt beneath the chapel. Carrying a votive with him to illuminate the steep and uneven steps, so he did not trip and break his neck, D'Artagnan, sword in other hand, descended into the noisome tombs. The glow of the candle revealed skulls grinning at him from crumbling alcoves. How many generations of the residents of Casale Monferrato found their final sleep in this crypt D'Artagnan could only imagine.

A low chanting came to his ears and to D'Artagnan's surprise it came from multiple voices. For some reason he had imagined that Martina was the sole worshiper of this Resheph, who she had proclaimed the god of plague and destruction. Of course, that made little sense. The footprints on the crates beneath the window had been of varied sizes, indicating more than just the matched feet of twin sisters.

D'Artagnan continued to thread his way through the labyrinth of the dead. The very walls, in some places, were built of bones which had fused together over the centuries, and the young musketeer imagined he was treading the very depths of hell. Finally, by following the murmurs of the chanting—which were repeated in some ancient tongue with which he was unfamiliar—he came to a low circular chamber some thirty feet across, which was edged by a multitude of crypts where moldered the remains of many a family.

A central crypt supported the ceiling of the chamber, but the bricks at the front of this crypt had either fallen away or been removed, so that it was open to the passage in which D'Artagnan paused, hidden in the shadows at its mouth. He extinguished the votive with a puff of breath, so that his position would not be revealed to the dozen revelers who repeated their monotonous dirge, swaying back and forth in robes which had apparently been stolen from the former priests of this church and been desecrated with the unholy symbol of Resheph .

The slab where once had lain the body of some ancient forefather of Casale Monferrato was now occupied by the Countess Ludovica Bianchi whose limbs were cinched tight with corded belts that had once adorned the vestments of priests. Beyond her, overlooking the scene with blind stone eyes, was a crudely hewn depiction of a slender Egyptian man holding a bow—Resheph, the god of plague and pestilence, who cast these as arrows.

A hooded figure bearing a dagger stood over the writhing Ludovica, who struggled vainly against the bonds which bit into her flesh. When the hooded figure spoke, D'Artagnan immediately recognized the voice of his lover, Martina. The assemblage did not cease to voice their chant, but they reduced the volume to a low murmur as the self-appointed priestess of Resheph spoke.

"Oh, God of Plague and Destruction, hear our prayers now and accept our sacrifice—and particularly my own sacrifice, the sacrifice of my own flesh whose blood will wet your altar and bring forth the last days before thy coming, which has been prophesied in the Tablets of Elba to be heralded by the Spreading Plague which will slay all the unbelievers and leave their rotting corpses heaped upon the streets of all lands and all nations!"

As D'Artagnan understood it from his late night conversations with Aramis, who knew about religion, this wicked ceremony was a bizarre perversion of the sacrifice of God's own son, who willingly laid down his own life, sacrificing his own flesh and blood to atone for the sins of the world and overcome both death and sin.

In this case, Martina was in a sense sacrificing her own flesh and blood because it was her sister, with whom she had shared the womb, who she was offering up—but by Ludovica's echoing screams it was apparent she was not willingly going to her death on this makeshift altar to Resheph.

And the second coming of which Martina said was prophesied by the Tablets of Elba, was also a corruption of the prophecies of many an Old Testament prophet, and of Christ Himself, who foretold that in the Last Days he would return, overthrow the wicked and come in his glory to usher in a millennium of peace and prosperity for the righteous. Instead, these tablets said it was Resheph who would come and overthrow the righteous with plague.

These were all thoughts that flashed through D'Artagnan's mind in a random disjointed fashion, but all these were overridden by the knowledge he must do something to save Ludovica. Though D'Artagnan could at times be crafty and subtle his hot temper often spurred him to rash action, and so it was the same now. Without judging whether he might be able to overcome the odds which seemed to be stacked insurmountably against him, he rushed out into the crypt.

He stifled a cry which he thought might serve to warn these enemies and instead burst into their midst, thrusting the tip of his rapier through the throat of the nearest cultist, so that he went down, clutching at his neck and gurgling out something incomprehensible. Before the other cultists realized what was transpiring, he thrust his blade through the heavy robes and into the spleen of a second of the unholy worshipers.

A third cultist went down grabbing at his face, which D'Artagnan slashed open with a wild swing. Before the rest of the cultists could fall upon him and rend him limb from limb in their unrighteous fury, D'Artagnan leaped to the slab where Ludovica Bianchi was restrained. He cut at one of the cords, loosening her right arm and then the musketeer realized he may

...he thrust his blade through the heavy robes...

have made a fatal mistake in directing his attentions first to Ludovica's bonds and not the High Priestess of Resheph.

Martina had not come unarmed to the worship. Besides the dagger which she held, she had thrust one of the Count Bianchi's pistols through the belt of her robe. She reached to the small of her back, and withdrew it even as she levered back the hammer of the flint. For a moment the gaping maw of the barrel pointed at D'Artagnan's face.

"I wager you didn't remember how to properly load the pistol," said D'Artagnan.

"Oh, poor D'Artagnan," replied Martina. "Do you really think you were the first man to ever show me how to load a firearm?"

She pulled the trigger as D'Artagnan jerked his head to one side. The concussion of the pistol deafened and singed the musketeer's left ear. Black gun smoke billowed into the air.

D'Artagnan did not bother to knock aside the pistol that had nearly slain him, for it was useless now except as a club to bludgeon him. That might indeed prove dangerous enough, but it was the dagger in Martina's right hand that concerned him most. It slashed at him and he managed to block the swing with a chop to Martina's wrist. Then he booted her away from the altar and into the wall of the crypt with such force that she dropped her dagger and, at least for a moment, sat stunned against it.

The musketeer had no time to ensure Martina was entirely disarmed, nor to finish freeing the Countess Bianchi from her remaining bonds. He managed to shrug off a tackle of a cultist and drive the pommel of his sword into the sternum of another. D'Artagnan felt himself being restrained by a half dozen hands and with a wild wrench which took every bit of his fear-fueled strength, he broke free, twisted about and slashed with his sword, momentarily driving back the throng of cultists.

Though, fortunately, many of these appeared to be unarmed, some of them apparently had obtained weapons in the forms of knives and clubs. These, led to action by their fanatic fervor for Resheph and bolstered by the weapons in their grasps, cried out curses against the interfering musketeer and launched themselves at him.

D'Artagnan, now free of restraint, deftly cut across the wrist of one cudgel-bearing cultist, causing him to drop his weapon. He parried a thrusting dagger and quickly riposted with a strike between the fellow's ribs and into his vitals. This cultist gave a gasp as his heart was transfixed and slid off the musketeer's blade.

Suddenly, the courage went out of the remaining cultists and they fled like fleas from a drowning dog's back. In a moment the chamber was abandoned save for the slumped and bleeding forms of the dead and dying.

"Hold on for a moment," D'Artagnan said to Ludovica who panted heavily, exhausted from her futile efforts to break free of her unsevered restraints.

"I'm not going anywhere, D'Artagnan," she replied.

The musketeer cut free one of her arms and one of Ludovica's legs before the scuff of a footstep on the stone of the crypt caused him to wheel around, holding his sword ahead of him. It was a fortuitous movement, for at that very moment Martina, having recovered her senses and her dagger, had leaped at D'Artagnan with the intent of stabbing him in the back while his attention was diverted by rescuing her twin sister.

The momentum of Martina's leap carried her right onto D'Artagnan's sword, completely penetrating her body, so that the point emerged from her back. Unprepared for this, D'Artagnan had the sword wrenched out of his hand, and Martina fell heavily against the slab of the makeshift altar, her head impacting with an audible crack.

Whether she died in that instant or if her heart momentarily continued to beat D'Artagnan could not say. He retrieved his blade, and black blood spilled from Martina's body when he wrenched it loose. Once he finished freeing Ludovica, she pivoted into a sitting position and, mouth agape, stared at the lifeless form of her twin.

"I'm sorry," apologized D'Artagnan. "I was trying my best not to kill her."

"This is the second of my family I have lost in this accursed crypt," said Ludovica, finally. "I do not fault you."

"The Count Bianchi was the other you lost," presumed D'Artagnan.

"Yes, and it was at my own hand—though I suppose I should be confessing this to a priest rather than a musketeer, but I have not yet found the opportunity, being locked up in my own cellar."

D'Artagnan faltered. "At your own hand?"

"Yes," replied Ludovica. "There was little to attract me to the Count, but I was resolved to make the best of it and thought perhaps that love would eventually come if I did my duty as a wife and Countess—but I began to suspect there was another woman." She gestured to her slain sister. "I was not entirely wrong, but the truth was even worse than I suspected."

"Your husband was having an affair with your twin sister?" questioned D'Artagnan.

Ludovica nodded. "I didn't even know she was in Casale Monferrato. Last my family heard she had taken up with some cult in Venice and was living a dissolute life with artists and stage actors, and had spent the last of her inheritance. Imagine my surprise when I followed my husband one night into this very same abandoned church and caught him rolling with my sister in some obscene rite to Resheph, even while others watched their perversions."

D'Artagnan was baffled as to why a husband would feel the need to find love with the exact physical duplicate of his own wife, but then he failed to understand why there were those who chose to worship a god of plague; perhaps the obscene rites had a certain attraction. "Why did Martina leave the luxuries of Venice for Casale Monferrato?"

"She knew my husband was a wealthy man and desired to lure him away. This she managed to do well enough by enticing him into the worship of Resheph. As I hid in the shadows of the stair I heard them whispering of how they would lock me away and Martina would pose as his wife."

"And Martina killed the Count Bianchi after she took your place?" questioned the musketeer.

"In a fashion. It would be easy enough to blame her," said Ludovica as she chafed at her limbs, the circulation slowly returning, "but he died at my own hand. I was angry. As he and Martina climbed the stairs I leaped from hiding and shoved him down the stairs. I'm not sure what I hoped to accomplish, but he broke his neck on the steps and was crippled, unable to move his arms or legs. Martina smothered him then forced me at knife point into imprisonment in my own cellar, where I remained while she seduced the soldiers and nobles of Monferrato and soiled my reputation."

"I am sorry to have contributed to that besmirching of your reputation. Though I have never breathed word of it, the affair could not be entirely concealed from my associates. It was obvious to them from the very beginning that I had attracted the interest of a very lovely woman."

"Martina was always shameless in displaying her affections," replied Ludovica, and then with a bit of pride added, "I suppose I couldn't blame you for being seduced by her, given that she looks very much like me."

"Are you able to stand?" questioned D'Artagnan. "Perhaps we should depart before the cultists decide to lay an ambush for us."

Gingerly, Ludovica rose to her feet and found her tingling feet were able to hold her weight. "I may need to lean on you as we climb the steps, if you do not mind the imposition."

"Not at all," said D'Artagnan.

Ludovica shuddered as she glanced at the two foot high depiction of Resheph. "The very stone of it seems to radiate a sinister force."

D'Artagnan responded by kicking over the idol, so that it broke into pieces. It was a satisfying act, but did nothing to diminish the oppressive evil that lingered thick in the miasma of the crypts. Retrieving one of the tapers that lit the scene of what might have been Ludovica's sacrifice, if not for his timely intervention, D'Artagnan and the true Countess Bianchi climbed through the tarry shadows that webbed the stairs, and emerged from the desecrated chapel even as a wan light seeped into the sky, painting the fringes of the horizon with color.

There was no sign of the escaped cultists and in fact, over the next few days, fearful that they might be identified by the Countess Bianchi, they fled Casale Monferrato with their households and goods—for many of them were wealthy landowners or businessmen.

Though Ludovica Bianchi was very grateful to D'Artagnan for her rescue and always left him an open invitation to her home, that invitation did not extend to her bedchamber—nor did D'Artagnan attempt to seduce the Countess. In fact, his visits were infrequent because of his embarrassment at the awkward situation of having carried on an unfortunate and passionate affair with a wicked and false version of the Countess. His weaknesses, foibles, and sins were plainly revealed to the Countess and this made D'Artagnan uncomfortable.

It might have been just as well for the few remaining cultists to have hastily departed Casale Monferrato, for Governor Ricci's spies reported that the Duke of Guastalla had gathered three thousand Spanish allies and another two thousand troops from his Hapsburg allies and was returning for a second engagement.

"This is ill news." Perspiration began to appear on the high-domed forehead of the diminutive Governor Ricci. "Captain Montagne, his artillery, and his men have long departed us and we have only the small contingent of my own five hundred French and Italian troops to resist another siege."

"Don't let your courage fail you," admonished D'Artagnan. "We may not have the numbers of Duke Guastalla, but we haven't been idle in our preparations. While the siege has been lifted we've filled the storehouses of Casale Monferrato, strengthened the walls, and thanks to Athos, moved the gun emplacements so we can inflict many casualties on the enemy should they be so rash to storm the walls."

"But we will be facing ten times our number!" The Governor stood from behind his overburdened desk, which was covered with requisitions and reports from numerous sources. Still, despite the apparent mess, he could locate any paper you might ask for within seconds.

"Captain Montagne was not a humble man," replied D'Artagnan, "but he did deign share some of his mathematical wizardry with those who were intelligent enough to comprehend it, and those artillerymen will be lobbing chain-shot into the enemy hordes long before they ever reach us. And I've trained your musket-men to shoot thrice in a minute. The Spanish troops we saw were lucky to manage one shot every two minutes. Nothing is sure in war, Governor, but if God is willing to bless our efforts, I like our chances."

"Is there any area of our preparation where we are lacking?" questioned Governor Ricci.

D'Artagnan considered this. "We just received a large shipment of powder in from France. Right now it is being stored in the powder depot—all in one spot. I should like to separate the powder into several locations."

"Why so?" questioned the governor.

"We should have depots near each gun emplacement so runners can quickly supply them," figured D'Artagnan, "and also, should we have saboteurs among us, they will have much greater difficulty destroying our supplies if they are spread into different locations."

"You think we may have saboteurs?" questioned the governor.

"A pagan cult managed to drive out all the clergy from Casale Monferrato without anyone knowing of their existence," replied D'Artagnan, who had previously relayed the story of his misadventures to the governor.

The governor mopped his forehead with a handkerchief. "It is a difficult story to believe, but my mother always maintained there were witches and warlocks in the mountains who ate little children. Why not in the towns and cities as well? Though it galls me they escaped my notice and were able to proliferate their evil without hindrance—and that Madam Marchesi and the Count Pugliesi were among them. My mind, it boggles, at the very idea."

"They shouldn't be troubling us any longer," said D'Artagnan.

In the tense days that followed, everyone fearing to see the sight of the Duke Guastalla's troops on the horizon, their enemy never materialized. Finally, the word of one of Governor Ricci's spies came to him. "The Duke of Guastalla has brought his troops against the Duke of Nevers in Mantua. Even now he besieges Mantua!"

Governor Ricci looked upon D'Artagnan with something akin to surprise as he absorbed the words of the messenger. "I was sure the Duke would come against the Casale Monferrato."

"Perhaps his spies reported the improvements to our fortifications," replied D'Artagnan. "Perhaps he figured his casualties would be too high in taking our fortress and decided it better to go directly for the Duke of Nevers. If he can cut the head from the body there is no reason to assail the Casale Monferrato."

"Perhaps you are right," said Governor Ricci, "but I cannot afford to send the Duke of Nevers aid. To do so, would be to leave Casale Monferrato woefully and inexcusably undefended."

"I do not fault you for such sentiments," replied D'Artagnan. "It is your duty to defend the fortress Casale Monferrato and the inhabitants of your village. Me, however, it is my duty to defend all the holdings of the Duke of Nevers and so it is time for me to say farewell, Governor Ricci, and thank you for your kind hospitality these last months."

"Are you sure this is wise?" questioned Governor Ricci. "Mightn't you prefer to stay and defend the walls of Casale Monferrato?"

"It is not a matter of my preference," replied D'Artagnan. "It is a matter of my duty and at this point my duty clearly lies in Mantua with the Duke of Nevers."

"Even if that duty is tantamount to suicide?" questioned Governor Ricci.

"I have sworn to give my life in the service of King Louis and for the greater glory of France. If King Louis has determined that I can best serve the interests of France in the defense of the Duke of Nevers then I will prosecute my duty to the best of my ability—even if it should mean being laid low by the musket fire of Spanish and Hapsburg soldier alike."

"But you will be trying to reach the Duke of Nevers through five thousand men," protested Governor Ricci, who did not want to see the life of this brave and resourceful ally, and even friend, extinguished.

"I did not let a few enemies stop me from reaching your fortress, Governor Ricci," replied D'Artagnan. "I merely rode through their midst until I reached your wall. I shall do the same at Mantua."

"But your horse was shot from beneath you when you came to Casale Monferrato," Governor Ricci reminded D'Artagnan. "And there will be five times as many men at Mantua."

"Then it will be necessary for me to create five times as much confusion," said D'Artagnan. "And the reminder of my slain horse will encourage me to greater speed, so I might outrun the musket balls of the enemy."

"You can't outrun musket balls," protested the Governor.

"That I shall have to discover," replied D'Artagnan stubbornly.

Governor Ricci, seeing he could not dissuade the young Musketeer from doing what he perceived was his duty to die, sighed. "Do you still have that fine horse that the false Countess Bianchi gifted you?"

"Nay," replied D'Artagnan. "Well, yes. That is, when I discovered that Martina had gifted me property which did not rightfully belong to her, I returned it to the rightful Countess after I rescued her. She took it under great protest, and the next morning when I visited the stables to see if there might be another mount suitable for a musketeer, I found the horse was in its stall, just as if I had never returned it to the stables of the Countess Bianchi."

"I see," replied Governor Ricci. "It should be plain to you, D'Artagnan, that as a sign of her gratitude, the true Countess Bianchi should like you to keep the horse."

"I suppose," said D'Artagnan reluctantly. "But I received the horse under false circumstances."

"But it was re-gifted to you under legitimate circumstances by the rightful owner," suggested Governor Ricci. "It would be to offer an offense to the Countess Bianchi if you should refuse it or leave it behind. You absolutely must take it with you when you ride for Mantua."

"I suppose you are correct," replied the recalcitrant musketeer.

"Of course, I am correct!" Governor Ricci produced a quill, dipped it in the ink pot and commenced to scribe a notice. "This writ shall offer you access to whatever supplies you deem necessary—though I would be much honored if you should stay with us in Casale Monferrato. For, when Mantua falls, as it likely shall, the Duke of Guantalla will certainly turn his attentions in this direction."

"If Mantua falls," suggested D'Artagnan, "you should do your best to make your peace with Duke Guantalla, so that he might spare your town and its people."

It was three days hard riding through rugged landscapes and D'Artagnan found the roads swarming with Spanish and Hapsburg patrols who were on guard in case relief for the besieged Mantua might be coming from France or from Casale Monferrato.

D'Artagnan alleviated this potential problem by ambushing a pair of

Spanish outriders he heard galloping down the path. He tossed his cap into the roadway and, leading his fine horse into the brush and obscuring it behind a copse of trees, he waited until the riders appeared around a bend in the trail.

Still, he did not fire. When the riders drew closer they halted in the roadway to examine the chapeau.

"It looks French," spoke the first rider.

Before his companion could agree or disagree, D'Artagnan fired his musket, blowing the second outrider from his horse. The rider, who had observed the hat in the road might be of French origin, snatched at his pistol, but D'Artagnan had already risen to full height from behind the log which he had obscured himself. D'Artagnan fired the pistol and the second rider jerked from the impact of a lead ball in his shoulder and dropped his pistol before he could return fire.

Emerging from the brush, D'Artagnan scooped up the fallen Spanish pistol and caught the bridle of his enemy's horse before the stunned rider could urge his confused mount away. The pistol was already cocked and ready to fire, but before D'Artagnan could send a ball into the brain of the bleeding Spaniard, the wounded man spoke in a heavily accented French.

"Mercy, I beg of you. Spare my life, please!"

"And who are you that I should spare your life?" questioned D'Artagnan. "Are you some wealthy nobleman I can ransom back to his family for a great price?"

"I am Juan Escarra and I am but a humble man with only enough means to purchase the horse I ride upon and the weapons with which I serve my king."

"Then what benefit is it to me to let you live?" questioned D'Artagnan.

"Perhaps it is a favor I will one day be able to return," suggested Juan Escarra.

"That is a fine thing to say," replied D'Artagnan, "but what if the day should never come when our positions are reversed?"

Escarra grimaced in pain. "It shall certainly never come if you slay me, now. But if you let me live who knows what God shall bring to pass? At the very least, spare me so I may go home to my wife and children and praise the name of the merciful and noble French man that spared my life!"

This fine speech and being called noble did in fact prick D'Artagnan's vanity. "There is one problem with your suggestion. I embark on a delicate mission and if word of it reaches the Spanish forces I will surely be caught and killed."

"Then allow me to swear an oath to you that I will not breathe word of your presence," said Escarra.

"And how will you explain the death of your partner?" questioned D'Artagnan.

"I will say we were ambushed by bandits," said Escarra. "They are thick in these mountains and it will readily be believed by those I report to."

"And who do you report to?" asked D'Artagnan.

"I report to Don Gonzala Fernandez de Cordoba," replied Escarra. "The Governor of Milan, who has allied himself with the Duke of Guastalla who is the heir to the Duchies of Mantua and Monferrato."

D'Artagnan's face hardened. "Ah, and there is the bone of contention. The Duke of Nevers contests that assertion."

Escarra saw that perhaps he his words had diminished his chances for mercy. "As he should! And perhaps if he had approached the Holy Pope for permission before seizing the duchies first, he might have been given the dispensation and been recognized as the rightful ruler—but in the meantime such folks as us are left to spill each others blood."

"Then swear to me you will not betray me to your superiors," said D'Artagnan, "and I will let you go your way—but you must leave your friend."

"I should surely take him," objected Escarra, "so that he might receive a proper burial and not feed the plague that is spreading across the land."

"Plague?" questioned D'Artagnan. "What plague to you speak of?"

"A pox and a pestilence is sweeping through the Spanish and Hapsburg troops and, judging by the bodies thrown from the walls, through the city of Mantua as well. It came suddenly and dozens are dying daily."

D'Artagnan scowled. "I shall bury your friend here in the woods, but you shall not take him with you."

"Hah," said Escarra. "I see your reasoning. You do not wish to do dishonor my slain companion, you wish to take his clothes to disguise yourself as a Spanish outrider."

D'Artagnan was nonplussed to see his intentions were so transparent. "Climb down from your horse so I may check the severity of your wound. It would not do for me to spare your life and then have you bleed to death on your way back to camp."

With much pain, Escarra succeeded in dismounting. D'Artagnan stripped away Escarra's shirt and washed away the blood.

Escarra hissed. "That is a potent water you carry in your water skin."

"Not water, but wine from the well-stocked cellars of the Countess Bianchi," replied D'Artagnan.

"And this Countess, she is a beauty is she not?" questioned Escarra, even as the musketeer probed the wound.

"Perhaps you have seen her before?" replied D'Artagnan.

"No," admitted Escarra, "but I can see the distant look in your eye when you speak her name. Perhaps you had a broken love affair?"

"Something along those lines, but she turned out to be a different person than I thought," replied D'Artagnan.

"Isn't that often the way of love?" replied Escarra. "But when you find the right woman, there will be no heartbreak. Just bliss…"

Escarra broke off with a sharp hiss as D'Artagnan probed his wound and pried out a lead ball.

"You are lucky," said D'Artagnan. "The gunpowder was weak and the ball did not even strike the joint. I think you will survive, but you will most certainly have a scar as a result of my inexpert surgery."

"Or rather your expert marksmanship," replied Escarra.

D'Artagnan compressed the wound until the bleeding slowed.

"I shall not forget my oath," replied Escarra.

"It would be best if you forgot me completely," said D'Artagnan. "It would be better if not even a thought of King Louis' musketeer ghosted across your mind, lest word slip out in a careless moment or even in the deep of sleep."

"My thoughts are guarded most carefully," Escarra assured him. "Now, if you should like to reach Mantua with the least interference I suggest you take the path through Gazzuolo. There will be pickets posted, but use the password of 'Spanish Glory' and they will let you through."

Escarra rehearsed the question in Spanish and forced D'Artagnan to repeat the answer until he could say it without a trace of French accent. After Escarra bid him farewell, D'Artagnan changed into the garb of the slain Spanish outrider, obscuring his musketeer's uniform beneath. As he had promised Escarra, D'Artagnan buried the Spanish soldier he had slain.

At a fork in the road, D'Artagnan took the path through Gazzuolo and thrice he met sentries who challenged him in Spanish. He answered tersely, with no more words than 'Spanish Glory' lest his limited Spanish and French accent betray him for an interloper.

As he neared Mantua he could scent the smell of death upon the land, rising up in an execrable miasma from the vast encampments encircling the city. In full daylight he wound his way through the encampment, nodding at those of rank and ignoring everyone else. This audacious infiltration brought him all the way to the front lines where cannons were

...D'Artagnan buried the Spanish soldier he had slain.

mounted behind walls of earth which had been cast up as defenses. Noting a trio of plague victims being wrapped into white sail cloth, D'Artagnan slowed the pace of his horse until the victims had been carted away to be burned in the bonfires.

He dismounted and cut himself a piece of sail cloth which he tied to a pole, then he rode past the gun emplacements and directly into the barren no man's land between the walls of Mantua and the forces of Duke Guastalla that encircled the city.

A single musket shot sounded from the wall of Mantua's fortress, casting up a plume of dust where it struck ten yards in front of D'Artagnan. Now, the musketeer raised his makeshift white flag of truce and continued alone to the very walls of the city, where he called up to the curious soldiers that guarded the walls.

"I should like to speak with the Duke of Nevers," called D'Artagnan in French. "I have important information to share with him."

"You are not the same envoy who came to us three days ago," replied a suspicious soldier.

"Nor should I be...since I come from Monferrato to report on the disposition of the Duke of Nevers' distant holdings in his other duchy."

This intrigued the captain in charge of the wall's defenses enough to open up a redoubt and allow the lone rider inside. This redoubt was quite low, so D'Artagnan dismounted before entering, leading his horse through the heavy door which was quickly slammed shut and thrice barred behind him.

Now, much to the interest and amazement of the surrounding soldiers, D'Artagnan stripped away the costume of the Spanish outrider, revealing the regalia of King Louis' musketeers beneath.

Captain Esposito gaped in awe. "You are either the bravest man I have ever seen or an utter fool to have rode directly through the enemy encampments and to our walls! But I'm afraid your bravery is for naught, all you've done by coming is doom yourself to death by plague or by the hands of Duke Guastalla's combined forces."

"King Louis sent me to Italy to die of that much I am sure," replied D'Artagnan. "Who am I to disappoint my sovereign lord? At least I shall die in the service of the people of Mantua."

"How did you pass all the enemy pickets?" pressed Captain Esposito who, though not in the least reassured by D'Artagnan's resigned speech, was still wondering at the spectacular feat of passing through the enemy hordes unmolested.

"I know their password," replied D'Artagnan. "I suspect it will be changed shortly, once they realize it was no envoy of theirs who rode to the walls of Mantua, but I do suspect they will be confused for awhile yet. And it is not as though the password will work so easily in releasing us from the city as it did in allowing me to reach Mantua."

"I suspect the Duke of Nevers should like to speak with you immediately," said Captain Esposito.

"And I should like to speak to him," said D'Artagnan, "though I don't suspect I shall be able to offer him any hope but that of a glorious death— one that I myself hope to achieve in the coming days."

"As would every soldier," replied Captain Esposito, though he certainly would have preferred some hope of victory over meeting his demise on the point of a Spanish sword.

The stench of the plague hovered over the city of Mantua as Captain Esposito escorted D'Artagnan through the maze of streets and to ducal manse, which was surrounded by a hundred of his personal bodyguards— lest some enterprising assassin suddenly end the reign of the Duke of Nevers.

Nevers, a stolid man in his mid-fifties with a broad nose and quick eyes, sat in a council chamber and was attended by a handful of military leaders who hunched over maps and examined the geography of the surrounding land. A woman of five decades and fading beauty sat on a stool just a pace behind Nevers, keeping a sharp eye on the proceedings.

As they entered, Esposito nudged D'Artagnan, directing his attention to the woman whose beautifully structured face had taken on a weathered appearance, like an image chiseled from stone that had been exposed to centuries of storms. The wonderful lips and the high arching brows were still there, but lines that could not be concealed by powder and rouge had appeared. "The Duchess of Nevers is the driving force behind the Duke of Nevers rise to power. If it were not for the Duchess's thirst for position, he might have been content to remain a mere landowner in the Piedmont-Savoy territories of France."

D'Artagnan acknowledged this with a nod. "Men will dare much for the women they love."

"You couch your words admirably," murmured Captain Esposito. "More bluntly spoken, we lose all our senses and become utter fools."

The Duke of Nevers was speaking to his Generals and Captains and he was not pleased. "Our Italian allies from the Republic of Venice are utterly useless. They came at the urging of the Pope, who has offered me his tacit support, but their three thousand troops sit idly ten miles away and do not come to our aid. Our reserves are running low, and everyday the plague claims one hundred more of my soldiers and citizens. Guantalla need do nothing but wait for us all to die."

"The plague is rampaging through the enemy forces as well," interjected D'Artagnan, seeing an opportunity to introduce himself.

The Duke of Nevers jabbed a finger in D'Artagnan's direction. "You, who are you? Your dress marks you as one of the king's musketeers. Please tell me you are the head of an army of musketeers who has ridden to our aid!"

"I apologize, Duke," said D'Artagnan. "I have ridden hard from Casale Monferrato, but I am the only one."

The hope that momentarily flickered in the Duke's eyes was snuffed as quickly as it had kindled. "And just how did you manage to breach the enemy lines and reach Mantua, musketeer?"

"I posed as a Spanish soldier," answered D'Artagnan.

"Tell me, musketeer. How does the fortress at Casale Monferrato fare?"

"It is sparsely garrisoned, but its defenses have been improved, its supplies replenished, and its troops have been rigorously trained for its defense."

"And is the Duke Guantalla besieging Casale Monferrato as well as Mantua?" questioned the Duchess Nevers.

"No, Madame," replied D'Artagnan with a bow. "His forces are concentrated here this time."

The Duchess snapped her fingers. "Then there is your answer, husband. We pull the soldiers from Casale Monferrato and have them fall upon the rear of the forces besieging us here in Mantua!"

D'Artagnan could see a number of problems with this scenario, but being the newcomer he thought perhaps it wise to wait and see if someone else might voice those same opinions.

It was the Duke of Nevers, himself, who spoke. "There are not enough soldiers in Monferrato to make a difference. They might, with God's blessing, be enough to defend the walls of the fortress, but they are not sufficient to fight both the Spanish and the Hapsburgs in the open fields. No, the only hope we have is if the troops from Venice can be persuaded to come to our aid, instead of chewing the fat and licking their fingers around their campfires."

"They have no reason to fight," dismissed the Duchess. "Nothing but a vague statement of support from Pope Urban. They fear Hapsburg influence, but they are not directly threatened yet, so they bide their time and see how events will unfold."

"Perhaps," volunteered D'Artagnan, "I could once again pass through enemy lines and seek these Venetian soldiers out. Maybe I could persuade them to engage at least the Hapsburg forces. Perhaps tell them of the plans we uncovered of the Hapsburg forces moving onto Venice as soon as they have overthrown Mantua."

"But we haven't uncovered any such plans," replied the Duke of Nevers.

D'Artagnan shrugged diffidently. "Just because we haven't uncovered them doesn't mean they don't exist, Duke. And certainly the Venetians should be aware of these plans to take over their city so that they might have an opportunity to take action before they are flooded with enemy Hapsburg troops."

"They will require proofs," said the Duke of Nevers. "They will want to see the dispatches and seals. We have none of that."

"Perhaps you have a skilled artisan who might be able to craft such papers?" suggested D'Artagnan. "I saw a printing establishment with the name of Aurelio Osanna. Perhaps they might be able to supply the craftsmanship to create such proofs as might be required?"

The Duke of Nevers looked around his table of commanders and none voiced an objection to this bit of subterfuge. "Is there no one here who should like to speak against this idea?"

"We are desperate," answered Captain Esposito. "If the plague continues at the same rate we shall soon have too few men to defend Mantua."

The Duke directed his attention to D'Artagnan. "And you think you might be able to pass again through the enemy lines?"

"That I cannot say for sure," replied D'Artagnan. "For the nonce I know the password but as for how long that password will remain in force…"

The Duke of Nevers nodded to his financier, a string-thin fellow with an equally narrow face that was as somnolent as if he were attending a funeral. "Tabor, accompany this musketeer to the printers and see if you can engage their services to create some clever forgeries."

"Yes, Duke," replied Tabor. "We will accomplish the task."

"Oh, musketeer," said the Duchess of Nevers before he departed with the financier. "What, pray tell is thy name?"

"D'Artagnan," replied the musketeer.

"That name sounds familiar," she mused. "I believe I may have heard it in connection with the queen?"

It horrified D'Artagnan that tales of a mere flirtation with her majesty, one that had never reached fruition, might have reached ears an entire country away. Still, he did his best not to register his alarm. "I am her humble servant."

"Perhaps that is it," replied the Duchess. "You were assigned as one of her guard?"

"I was at one time," replied D'Artagnan. "Now, I am assigned to the service of the Duke and Duchess of Nevers."

The more D'Artagnan pondered the idea of returning through enemy lines by posing as a Spanish soldier, the more he didn't like it. The idea of repeating the same tactic galled him in two ways: one, that he had already accomplished the feat and it seemed uncreative to repeat the same exact tactic; two, that such a miraculous occurrence seemed unlikely to succeed twice.

For this reason, while the artisans at Aurelio Osanna worked on papers in German and sought to duplicate the Hapsburg seals, the musketeer wandered the perimeter of Mantua, studying the entrances, gates, and walls. He asked everyone he encountered about ways in and out of the city, and he finally made conversation with a pretty young Italian girl named Cynzia, daughter of a cheese maker who owned a shop at the city's edge—or at least what was now the city's edge. The Duke of Nevers had ordered many of the dwellings around the most easily fortifiable areas of Mantua razed to the earth so there might be a clear field of fire against the enemy.

"You must keep this a secret," said Cynzia who was very charmed by the handsome French musketeer, "but my father has a way out of the city. He has a cellar full of cheeses and in expanding it he accidentally broke through into a neighbor's cellar whose house once stood on the other side of the wall. Out of curiosity he continued digging, and found that this cellar adjoined another and another. We plan to flee this evening for lands that are not plague ridden or surrounded by hosts of the enemy. We have relatives in Milan and we can stay there. Perhaps you should like to come with us?"

"I would like that very much," replied D'Artagnan.

"I'm sure my uncle could find a place for you to sleep as well," said Cynzia, "should you like to come to Milan with us."

"That is a very generous offer," answered D'Artagnan, neither declining or accepting the offer. It seemed to D'Artagnan that the lively and pretty little Cynzia was hoping for a husband in the bargain, but if he dashed her illusions too early he might lose his escape route. "Where should I meet you?"

Cynzia pointed to a sparkling pool of water beneath the ivory arms of a statue raised to Aradia the witch goddess. "Meet me at the fountain just before the sun goes down and you shall come with us!"

She impulsively kissed D'Artagnan and then ran off, unable to hide her excitement. Indeed, D'Artagnan enjoyed the taste of her kiss and for a moment he wondered if he should accept the invitation of the spritely girl and leave behind the responsibilities of a musketeer. After all, hadn't King Louis exiled him from France in the hopes that he might die? Certainly, if he disappeared in the wilds of Italy, no one would miss him—except for perhaps the loyal Porthos, austere Athos, and godly Aramis.

Still, this moment of temptation fled from him. For D'Artagnan was above all loyal to his country, his friends, and the king. So if the king decided it was D'Artagnan's duty to die, then he would face that duty and die just as the king commanded. Time was running short, so he returned to the printing establishment of Aurelio and Ludovica Osanna, bursting into the back chambers where stood the mechanical presses and plates of type. These were being set by a number of apprentices, who were alarmed to see the musketeer barging into their workplace.

"I must speak with your masters, now!" said D'Artagnan.

"They are working in the back room on a project for a secret client," replied one of the trembling apprentices.

D'Artagnan presumed this secret client was the Duke of Nevers himself and so he did not hesitate to enter the back room, closing the door behind him so as to preserve the secrecy of their project. "I must have the papers before nightfall!" he announced to the balding Aurelio Osanna, who was bent over a document which he was carefully scribing.

"Magari!" Ossana threw up his hands. "This type of work takes great skill and time. It cannot be rushed. You will have your papers when we are finished and only when I am finished!"

"And you will be finished with it before nightfall," directed D'Artagnan.

"It cannot be done!" protested Ossana. "I will do the work properly and I will take the time necessary to do the work to my satisfaction."

"The window of opportunity will have passed if the work cannot be completed by sun fall," said D'Artagnan. "At the time darkness sets upon Mantua there will be no reason to complete the work. It will all be for naught."

"The craftsmanship of such a work is a reason unto itself," said Ossana. "There is pride in such artistry and I will not be rushed into producing an inferior product."

"Perhaps you do not understand the gravity of the project you have been asked to accomplish," replied D'Artagnan. "Your very own life and the existence of Mantua depends upon you swiftly completing the work. You are currently besieged, completely surrounded by Spanish and Hapsburg, and yet you pause to quibble with me about a few hours."

"Precisely," said Ossana, testily. "If you would leave me in peace I could go back to my work."

"Which must be completed before dusk!" reiterated D'Artagnan.

"I do not understand the urgency," said Ossana. "How are forged documents of a supposed invasion of Venice supposed to save Mantua?"

"That will be my task," said D'Artagnan. "Your task is to finish these documents be…"

"Before nightfall," finished Ossana. "It can't be done to my satisfaction."

D'Artagnan drew his sword. "It will be done, at least, to my satisfaction, even if I should have to hold the point of this blade to your neck at every stroke of your pen."

"If you slay me," said Ossana defiantly, "there will be no one who can finish this project."

"If you do not finish these papers this very day, there will be no reason for me to let you live," replied D'Artagnan.

Ossana swallowed hard, realizing he had met his match in stubborness. "Very well, I will finish the papers—but I cannot guarantee their perfection under such circumstances."

"They don't need to be perfect," replied D'Artagnan, leaving his blade unsheathed. "They just have to be sufficient to fool the eyes of a Venetian General."

Despite the bitter complaints of Aurelio Osanna, the printer did finish forging the documents—though he warned at least a dozen times that they were not done to the standards of his satisfaction.

"Pray they are done well enough," D'Artagnan told him. "The safety of your family may depend upon them."

When D'Artagnan bid goodbye to the Duke and Duchess of Nevers, the Duke was receiving the grim news that the number of his forces had fallen to eight hundred.

"We scarcely have enough men left to guard the gates and the causeways," warned Captain Esposito. "Another day or two of plague and we won't even have sufficient numbers to accomplish that. Already we've run out of wood to burn the bodies of the plague victims and so we are forced to weight the bodies and sink them in the lake."

"Surely the Duke Guastalla's forces must be daily losing men as well," said the Duke of Nevers.

"They are," agreed Captain Esposito. "Their bonfires burn bodies day and night, but they started with many more men than we did."

The Duke of Nevers turned upon D'Artagnan. "You have two days to persuade the Venetians to come to our aid. If they cannot drive off the Spanish and Hapsburg forces, we shall have no other option but surrender."

"Better we all die fighting or from the plague," said Captain Esposito. "Count Johann Von Aldringen is in charge of the Hapsburg troops. If we surrender or are captured alive, he will have us drawn and quartered or order our intestines pulled from our body so that we die slowly in great agony."

The Duchess covered her face with her begemmed fingers when she heard this, crying out in dismay at the fate that awaited her.

"Give me three days," requested D'Artagnan. "I am a man of meager wit but great determination, and I will find a way to persuade the Venetian general to come to your aid."

"Pray that it is enough," said the Duke of Nevers. "Pray that it is enough."

The beautiful Cynzia awaited D'Artagnan beneath the outstretched ivory arms of the witch goddess, who presided in stony splendor over the fountain. She fell trembling into the musketeer's strong arms. "I was so worried that you might not come!"

"How could I resist an invitation to accompany you from the city?" replied D'Artagnan. "Your face has never left my mind since we last parted."

"You shall find Milan an agreeable city in which to make a home," said the eager Cynzia.

D'Artagnan did not want to yet reveal to her that he would not be accompanying her to Milan. He felt bad for letting her believe the story she had concocted in her mind of escaping Mantua with a handsome musketeer, with who she would start a family in the great city of Milan. "I hear it is a fine place."

"The most wonderful," agreed Cynzia, showering him with kisses.

D'Artagnan found his reluctance was quickly overcome by the passion of the moment, but finally he was forced to urge Cynzia to seek out her family. "Your father and your mother will be worried about you. Do they know I will be accompanying them?"

Cynzia hesitated and then admitted, "I have not yet told them of you."

"Just as well," replied D'Artagnan. "They will not have much time to object to my presence."

"I'm sure they will grow to love you—just as I have!" assured Cynzia.

She spoke with the passion of youth, which D'Artagnan had not long ago experienced for himself when he had fallen into the embrace and clutches of the Milady DeWinter. Cynzia had known D'Artagnan only for hours, yet already she was convinced they had family and future together in the idyllic city of Milan, whose forces were even now encamped about Mantua, threatening to lay waste to it and all of its inhabitants.

"Lead the way," urged D'Artagnan. "I am very anxious to meet your parents."

He followed Cynzia through a maze of homes, some of which showed the marks of cannon fire. Indeed, some of the homes had been leveled by the enemy bombardment and were little more than a pair of crumbling walls, the rest having been pounded into rubble.

The home of Cynzia's parents had survived with just a few pockmarks upon the walls. A broken sign hung above the door, marking this as the residence of a maker of fine cheeses. Churns and vats stood empty in the back gardens. As soon as Cynzia stepped through the front door, she was rushed inside by her overwrought and gray-haired mother.

"Cynzia! We didn't know what had happened to you! You shouldn't be abroad with the plague ravaging the city!"

"I was merely fetching a drink of water from the fountain and filling the skins for our trip." Cynzia displayed the full skins she had brought home, and D'Artagnan demonstrated a half dozen full skins which he also carried.

"Who is this...this Frenchman?" questioned Signor Russo, a once stout cheese maker whose paunch had dissipated in the lean days that were upon Mantua. "Why did you bring him to our home?"

"He knows, father! He knows we are leaving Mantua and he wants to come with us!" cried Cynzia.

"He knows," repeated Signor Russo. "Then I suppose we have no choice but to bring him along. It wouldn't do for word to spread, or the Duke of Nevers' soldiers might collapse our tunnels before we can use them to escape."

D'Artagnan knew this was far from a wholehearted endorsement by

Signór Russo, but it was enough.

"What possessed you to tell him of our plan, Cynzia?" questioned Signór Russo.

"Isn't it obvious enough?" replied Signóra Russo. "Our daughter has found a handsome suitor."

"A suitor?" scoffed Signór Russo. "We know nothing of him. And he is a Frenchman!"

"Against that accusation I have no defense," answered D'Artagnan, "and there is no point in denying it. I am a proud Frenchman."

"It is because of the French we are in this predicament," grumbled Signór Russo. "If King Louis did not so badly want our territory we should not be besieged by Duke Guantalla and his Hapsburg mercenaries!"

"King Louis wanted nothing to do with this territorial squabble," answered D'Artagnan. "He already had his hands full of Huguenots and wanted to stay clear of Italy, but when he heard Spain had their eyes on Mantua and Monferrato he—or more likely the Cardinal Richelieu—felt he had no choice but to get involved."

"But not involved enough," said Signór Russo. "The French leave us to be consumed by plague or foreign armies."

"Which is it?" questioned D'Artagnan, who had just heard two opposing arguments against France. "Should the French not have become involved or should they be involved?"

"Halfway is not a position any country should take," replied Signór Russo, finally.

"Upon that much we can agree!" said D'Artagnan. "Now, I have a sword which I will be pleased to use in the defense of your family should we encounter Spanish or Hapsburg soldier in our escape. At least, this particular Frenchman may prove of some use to you."

"Do not use your sword," directed Signór Russo. "I may be able to talk our way through the lines."

"Really?" replied D'Artagnan, who began to suspect this might not be the first time Signór Russo had used the tunnel. "And what will you tell them?"

"Leave that to me," said Signór Russo.

"It is preferable to use a quick tongue over a quick sword," agreed the musketeer. "Yet, I find a quick sword is a valuable resource when words fail—which they often do."

"Whatever you do, do not draw your sword unless I give you the signal," reiterated Signór Russo.

"And what will be that signal?" questioned D'Artagnan.

"You will know when the time comes," replied Signor Russo, most unhelpfully.

D'Artagnan raised his eyebrow. "I suppose I shall, at that."

Signor Russo barred the doorway to his cottage. "Dusk is falling. It will take some time for us to work our way through the tunnels, and I should like to be in position to leave them once darkness has completely fallen."

D'Artagnan had absolutely no objection to this, so he shouldered the water skins along with a rucksack of his own supplies and descended a narrow passage into the Russo's cellar. The many shelves which had once been full of aging cheeses were empty except for nigh on twenty blocks. Signor Russo packed these into a small handcart.

"I can pull the cart for you," offered D'Artagnan, who could see wheel tracks leading through a hole in the far end of the cellar. This was more proof that the cart had been used through this tunnel system before. Probably, Signor Russo had been selling cheese to enemy troops at high prices, as well as benefiting from a scarcity of food and the exorbitant prices inside Mantua.

"It may be helpful after all to have a young man along," said a grudging Signor Russo.

"I'll light the way with a lantern." Holding the oil light aloft Cynzia forged ahead through the series of interconnected cellars.

D'Artagnan realized they were passing beneath the very wall of Mantua and then beneath the Spanish and Hapsburg encampments. Indeed, he could hear the murmur of voices emanating through the earth so that they were a faint rumble in his ears. They stepped carefully, D'Artagnan painfully aware of the crunch of the cart's wheels over the debris of the broken foundations.

Eventually, their progress came to an end and there was no egress except for a hole in the floor of the cellar. D'Artagnan could see that a ramp of earth had been cast up so that the cart could be rolled down the slope.

"Where does it lead?" asked the musketeer.

The cheese maker replied. "It is an ancient aqueduct made by our forefathers, but it has since dried up. There are not enough cellars for us to travel beneath all the enemy lines. Even this aqueduct will not take us completely beyond them."

"And if we meet the enemy?" questioned D'Artagnan.

"Let me handle that problem," said Signor Russo.

"Very well," replied D'Artagnan. "I can see that this is not the first time

D'Artagnan...descended a narrow passage into the Russo's cellar...

you have traveled this route."

"No," admitted Signòr Russo. "I have traded with the Hapsburg soldiers before to provide necessities that were running short within Mantua."

D'Artagnan did not condemn the man for trading with the enemy. A few blocks of cheese were not going to cause the forces of the Duke of Guantalla to overwhelm Mantua. That die had been cast well before and would not be weighted by such a miniscule contribution. He eased the cart down the tenuous ramp of loosely packed earth, the wheels sinking and slowing his descent so he was not overrun by the cart.

The aqueduct beneath was bone dry and the wheels passed over the ancient brickwork with ease. Tiny eyes reflected in the light of Cynzia's lantern, but these denizens of the dark were frightened by the human interlopers and fled into shadow and hole.

They traveled for sometime, D'Artagnan pulling the cart up the long slopes into impenetrable darkness until, finally, the aqueduct ended in a cave in that caused them to emerge into a stand of trees thick with foliage. This last slope required the help of Signòr and Signòra Russo to help push the cart out, because it was so heavily laden with the family's worldly belongings.

D'Artagnan paused to catch his breath and when he gazed out from the copse of trees he found they were in the outer edges of the Spanish forces. All around them glittered the campfires of the enemy, smoke wafting to their nostrils, and snatches of conversation drifting to their ears through the calm of the night.

"None of the soldiers know that we come from Mantua," spoke Signòr Russo as he took care to obscure the entrance to the aqueduct with a pile of brush. "They think we journey from a nearby town to sell my cheese."

"And how will you explain me?" said D'Artagnan. "The presence of a French musketeer will surely cause some suspicion."

"Change into some of my clothing," said Signòr Russo. "I will tell them you are my son-in-law."

This suggestion delighted Cynzia, who perhaps thought a bit of play-acting the part might prepare D'Artagnan for just such an eventuality.

"My Italian is poor," warned D'Artagnan. "And my Spanish will surely reveal my French accent and betray me."

Signòr Russo patted the musketeer on his broad shoulders. "I shall tell them you are my mute son-in-law. That will relieve you of having to speak a word."

D'Artagnan stepped behind a tree and changed into a set of Signòr Russo's clothing. Signòr Russo was shorter and heavier than the musketeer, so the pants were embarrassingly short and the fit quite baggy. Still, D'Artagnan resolved to the play the part convincingly. To better play the part of a wife, Cynzia took him by the arm even as he pulled the cart loose from the underbrush and into the surrounding Spanish encampment.

"I should love you even if you were mute," Cynzia whispered to him.

Perhaps even more, thought D'Artagnan. For then he would not be able to tell her the unfortunate news that he would not be accompanying her or her family to Milan as she had led herself to believe.

It wasn't long before they encountered Spanish soldiers who roughly accosted them, but once Signór Russo explained he was a simple cheese maker selling his wares, as well as a couple bottles of wine from his personal reserve, he had a number of Spanish soldiers offering every coin they had, and even the cartridges for their rifles in exchange for the alcohol.

The cheese was popular too, for food was perpetually short outside the walls as well as within Mantua. However, the prospect of tippling far outweighed the prospect of a full belly in the minds' of many of the soldiers. As a result, Signór Russo was able to turn a handsome profit and leave the encampment without any hindrance.

At first, some of the soldiers had considered D'Artagnan with suspicion, but once Signór Russo explained the young man was his mute son-in-law they mostly ignored him, and it was if he didn't even exist—at least to the soldiers. Cynzia, however, caught many admiring and lustful glances and she might have been at hazard if she had not clung so tightly to D'Artagnan, who silently observed the bargaining.

Once they were well away from enemy lines, Signór Russo let out a low chuckle. "God is with us this evening. We have made our escape from the very midst of a vast host of enemy."

"And I have gained a fiancee!" announced Cynzia.

D'Artagnan was even more surprised at this pronouncement than Signór Russo. Signóra Russo, however, did not seem too alarmed at the idea, for Cynzia had inherited from her mother the brash ability to set her sights on a man and presume upon him until her wishes became a reality.

However, the musketeer had never proposed marriage to Cynzia. Though he did not fail to find favor in the peasant girl's leggiadrous form, he had been recently involved in a romance with a supposed Countess and before that in a flirtation with the Queen of France herself, and so it might be forgiven him if he thought perhaps the prospect of marriage to the daughter of a cheese maker a bit mundane. Nor did he have the desire to settle down to the task of raising a family, when perhaps he might rejuvenate his prospects as a musketeer to the Royal Court of France if only he could persuade the Venetian forces to come against the besiegers of Mantua.

"I am afraid," replied D'Artagnan, "that I will not immediately begin to pursue my suit of marriage to your lovely daughter. I first have duties to the throne of France which I must complete."

This was just fine with Signór Russo, who was not at all anxious to see his daughter married to a French man—no matter how skilled he might be at pulling a cart or playing a mute. Still, it might be nice to have someone else to pull the cart on the long trip to Milan. "That is unfortunate. Once we are in Milan, perhaps I can introduce you to people who might be able to aid you in your endeavors."

"Sadly, I must part ways with you, and your lovely wife, and daughter much sooner," said D'Artagnan. "I am on an urgent business for the Duke of Nevers and…"

Cynzia threw herself upon the musketeer. "But D'Artagnan, I cannot bear to be parted! My soul should wither and die should I be out of your presence for more than a day!"

The young, D'Artagnan knew, felt all emotion very keenly, for he was not far removed from this vast magnification of all feelings. "And I too shall count the moments we are parted in the hopes that soon our beggared souls will be reunited. I will find you in Milan once my duties here are accomplished!"

"Do you swear it?!" Cynzia clutched at her breast. "Oh, swear you will find me once you have accomplished your duty to your king!"

D'Artagnan took her trembling hand and clutched it to his heart, caught up in the fervor of her emotion. "I swear it, Cynzia."

They traveled on that same path for hours and then settled down for the evening. In the morning their paths would diverge and D'Artagnan would seek out the Venetian hosts and discover if his skills at subterfuge and persuasion were up to the task he had set for himself.

Not long after he went to sleep he heard a sweet voice whispering in his ear and felt the tickle of golden locks upon his face.

"D'Artagnan," whispered Cynzia. "It is I, your beloved!"

"What is it?" questioned D'Artagnan as he grasped for his sword, thinking perhaps that they were about to be overwhelmed in a host of the enemy.

"My parents sleep," whispered Cynzia. "I should like to give you something I have never given to any man before."

Immediately, D'Artagnan was completely awake, and the closeness of Cynzia's body to his awoke a passion and desire he had not felt since his nights with the false Countess. Still, he could not bring himself to take what Cynzia was offering under the false pretenses he would seek her out in Milan and marry her. True enough, he had taken an oath to find her in Milan once his duties were performed, but despite her desirability he had no intention of asking for her hand in marriage, and so to take her innocence seemed a heinous thing to do.

True, he had willingly enough gone to Martina Bianchi's bed, but she had no expectations but a night of pleasure—and even so he felt guilty about that, wondering if it was because of his sin that the plague had descended upon Mantua.

"I do not want to spoil you for the marriage bed," replied D'Artagnan, finally. "It will be a sweeter thing if we should wait, instead of taking stilted pleasure while your parents sleep a few paces away. Think what should occur if they should happen to awake."

Passion tended to fog one's reason to risks and consequences, but this last argument reluctantly persuaded Cynzia of the wisdom of waiting. "Promise me you will come to Milan just as soon as is humanly possible!"

"I will," replied D'Artagnan, simultaneously wondering how, at that time, he was going to spoil her expectations without causing her leap broken-hearted from a high tower.

The next morning, sweet kisses still tingling on his lips, D'Artagnan parted ways with the Russo family. Shortly after, he encountered a Hapsburg outrider who he slew with a thrust through the ribs and into the heart. Once the outrider had finished dying, D'Artagnan placed the documents forged by the printer Aurelio Osanna in the dead man's breast pocket.

He slung the man over the back of his own horse and climbed into the slain Hapsburg outrider's saddle. The horse, showing no loyalty whatsoever to his former master, willingly bore D'Artagnan at a blistering clip toward the Venetian encampment.

In his sprawling and well furnished tent, the tall and whipcord slender General DeLucca, who presided over the three thousand idle Venetian soldiers, examined the forged documents for at least the tenth time. "I can't believe it," he repeated.

"And why not?" asked D'Artagnan. "Isn't the evidence right before your very own eyes? The Hapsburg soldiers plan to fall upon Venice immediately after they have razed Mantua. What is there not to believe?"

"I find it hard to believe the treachery and double dealings of Count John von Aldringen, who having the unmitigated gall to stand before me in this very tent, swore he had no designs upon Venice, and offered me a coffer of gems and gold as a symbol of his goodwill!"

"As a bribe!" interjected D'Artagnan. "It was not a symbol of his goodwill, but rather a bribe to induce you to sit on your hands while he maneuvered his troops into taking an only partially defended Venice. There are his orders, signed in his own hand, to his own commanders, that they should be prepared to fall upon Venice just as soon as the looting of Mantua was finished! What more evidence of his perfidy could you ask?"

"None, I suppose," replied General DeLucca whose face grew purple with anger at being misled and betrayed by the Count John von Aldringen.

"Then the question I humbly put forth to you," said D'Artagnan in his most mild manner, lest he overplay his hand, "is are you going to let this bald-faced liar remain unpunished for his mendacity?"

For tenuous moments all D'Artagnan's schemes hung in balance as the weak-willed and corrupt General DeLucca, a man who had been bought by a chest of baubles from the Count John von Aldringen, considered the evidence of betrayal that the musketeer had brought to him. Would he be so incensed that his family and hometown of Venice was in danger that he would be pushed to action or would his cowardly nature hold sway and cause him to delay?

As DeLucca stewed in indecision, D'Artagnan decided to appeal to the General's vanity. "You will certainly be safer if you stay camped right here, but imagine what people will say if they learn the great General DeLucca allowed himself to be made a goat and did not rise to defend his own reputation."

This was a dangerous thing to say, for it would be an easy thing for the General DeLucca to vent his spleen on D'Artagnan who was standing right in front of him. A few words from General DeLucca's lips and D'Artagnan might shortly be standing before a firing squad of Venetian soldiers.

It appeared the General DeLucca was on the verge of ordering just such a thing when he paused mid-word. "My men are ready to fight and avenge this insult!"

To D'Artagnan this was still not conclusive enough a statement, for General DeLucca might have been saying that the musketeer had insulted him. However, D'Artagnan chose to presume that DeLucca was speaking of the insult that had been offered by the Count John von Aldringen's imagined betrayal. "If I may make a suggestion, wise General: the best time to strike at the Hapsburg armies is while they are besieging Mantua, their soldiers facing the city and their flanks exposed to a surprise attack. If your armies delay for too long the Hapsburg soldiers will soon have the walls of Mantua as a defense and then the cost of defeating them will be much higher—best to take advantage of them and pin them between two enemies."

This appealed to General DeLucca's conservative nature, for he little liked risks. In truth, D'Artagnan judged that the Hapsburg and Spanish forces were not entirely undefended on their flanks, for despite the deal they had made with General DeLucca they had not entirely put their faith in his cowardice and his willingness to shirk his duty for jewels and Italian coin. They had at least mounted some defenses at the rear of their encampment. Still, D'Artagnan did not feel it wise to mention these facts lest General DeLucca's anger become tempered by the reality that even a rear attack upon a force that was over twice as large might not route the enemy.

General DeLucca slammed his fist upon the arm of his divan. "We go to war! Order the men to readiness. We leave at first light to crush the lying dogs who thought to make fools of General DeLucca and the Venetian people!"

Seeing that his appeal to the pride of the General DeLucca had stirred the Venetian general into action, D'Artagnan allowed himself the slightest of smiles. He slept a fitful night in a small tent allotted for the use of visitors, and in the morning D'Artagnan surveyed the Venetian troops with great disappointment. They were poorly trained, unevenly marshaled and they lacked any sort of bombardment capabilities. The one six-pound cannon they had was on a broken carriage and could not be brought along to the battle.

As they marched toward Mantua, D'Artagnan noticed the crooked ranks and the laggards who fell out along the wayside and were whipped back into place by captains and lieutenants who had their hands full in attempting to maintain some semblance of order. In general it seemed that the Venetian troops lacked the discipline and fire of the French...or for that matter, the Spanish or Hapsburg soldiers he had encountered in his travels through their lines.

To firm their resolve, D'Artagnan told stories of rapine and deturpation which would doubtless be inflicted upon Venice should the Hapsburg soldiers fall upon that city. Though D'Artagnan had no actual knowledge that the Hapsburgs had designs upon Venice, he spoke of it as an inevitable thing if they were not stopped at Mantua. And why not? For he had no knowledge that it wasn't true—and just because he wasn't sure that Count Johann von Aldringen had designs upon Venice didn't mean that the Hapsburg count didn't.

Like any army, the Venetian soldiers loved a good rumor and so the stories D'Artagnan told spread like the plague through the ranks. These fired the soldiers to righteous anger, stoking their will and courage to do battle. It did nothing for the lack of discipline within the Venetian ranks, but there was little that a lone French musketeer could do in less than a day to resolve that problem.

Still, when the Venetians first met and captured Hapsburg scouts it was all General DeLucca could do to keep his soldiers from slicing off their heads and mounting them on pikes at the forefront of the Venetian army, so enraged were the soldiers at what the Hapsburg army intended for the women and children of Venice—for the stories had grown so horrific in the telling that D'Artagnan scarcely recognized them anymore by the time they again reached his ears.

Fortunately, General DeLucca was able to rescue these Hapsburg pickets, before they were torn limb from limb, and he put them to questioning. Considering the fate they had narrowly escaped, these Hapsburg pickets were eager to cooperate and readily answered every query put to them, providing troop strength and positioning to the best of their meager knowledge.

Unfortunately, the advance of the Venetian troops did not go entirely unnoticed and word did reach the Count Johann Von Aldringen just prior to the arrival of General DeLucca's forces. So, the Hapsburg forces were in the process of turning around to protect their flanks when the Italian forces burst upon them. The Venetians initiated the conflict by pouring a ragged sleet of musket fire into the rotating Hapsburg ranks.

Dozens of Hapsburg soldiers crumpled in this initial volley, and if the Venetians had been trained to speedily reload they might have withheld two wings of musketry in which they could have pounded and restrained the Hapsburg lines in continuous volleys. However, all discipline was lost after this early volley and the Venetian soldiers, inflamed with righteous rage, poured down the slopes with bayonet, pikes and sword.

D'Artagnan found himself swept up in this wave of charging men and so he shouted encouragement and galloped his horse into the forefront of the rush. Musket balls whipped at his clothing. A few Venetians stumbled and were trampled by their fellows who could or would not halt their headlong rush to meet the hated Hapsburgs.

By fate or fortune D'Artagnan was unwounded by the Hapsburg volleys and moments later his horse leaped the earthen emplacement of a cannon being charged for use against the Venetians. He trampled one of the hapless gunners and put his pike through the chest of the gunnery sergeant who cried out curses, clutching at the pole in his chest even as he reeled to the earth.

The Countess Bianchi's horse could not quell its excitement and continued his wild gallop into the midst of the Hapsburg soldiery. The Venetians took heart at seeing this brave musketeer charge so recklessly into the enemy ranks and they followed with lusty cheers, chopping down any luckless Hapsburg soldier who happened into their path.

Finding no reason to check his galloping horse, D'Artagnan trampled Hapsburg soldiers into the muck and mire, cleaving neck and face at every stroke as he leaned low to avoid the constant gunfire. Fortunately, now that he was in the thick of the enemy, the Hapsburg musketry was not able to focus their fire upon him for fear of hitting their own men.

The Hapsburg musket men were well trained and capable of putting up a wall of withering fire against any enemy who had not reached them. However, their ranks had not been completely set when the Venetians had come upon them and so they were not able to use their muskets to their usual great effect, because the angry Italians were soon among them, chopping and clubbing. The battlefield devolved into clumps of wild melee where Hapsburg and Venetian entirely lost their ranks and were mixed in violent gallimaufrey.

Never did D'Artagnan lose his momentum. His horse trod the enemy beneath its hooves, and its rider was lost in a swirl of savage faces, striking at all unfortunate enough to come within reach of his blade. His boots were cut to ribbons by slashing enemies and his horse's flanks were spattered with the blood of Hapsburg and then Spaniard as he broke through the soldiers belonging to the Count John Von Aldringen.

A knot of Venetian soldiers came in D'Artagnan's wake, slaying those he had wounded or crushed into the mire, and killing those along the periphery. And so they miraculously advanced all the way through the enemy lines and to the very walls of Mantua. Suddenly, D'Artagnan was surprised to find his way blocked by a wall and found there was no more enemy to kill. When he wheeled his horse about, he found that seven hardy Venetians had made the entire journey with him.

There had been at least three score with D'Artagnan when first he breached the enemy line. The others had fallen along the way. In looking to see how the forces of General DeLucca had fared against the besiegers, he was disappointed to see that the Venetian ranks had had collapsed and were fleeing the field of battle. D'Artagnan's efforts had not been enough to overcome the poor discipline and generalship of DeLucca's Venetian army.

D'Artagnan's elation at having fought completely through the enemy lines dissolved when he saw that he would not obtain victory this day. He also considered that he might not live to fight another day, because a squad of two score Spaniards was venturing after D'Artagnan and his seven bold and brave Venetians.

Before the Spaniards could reach them, however, a cannon ball plowed through their ranks, chopping four men asunder. Another cannon fired from the wall and this caused three men to dissolve in a spray of blood. The musket men on Mantua's wall took up the deadly refrain, their weapons bellowing flame and smoke, and lead balls mowing down the enemies who dared venture too close to the wall.

A redoubt opened in Mantua's walls and under the cover of the musket men on the walls, D'Artagnan and his seven Venetians entered the dubious safety of the city.

When D'Artagnan went before the Duke and Duchess of Nevers he was inconsolable at his failure to wrest Mantua from the clutches of the enemy. "I have failed you, Duke. I beg your humble forgiveness, if you can find it in your heart to excuse my ineptitude."

"Nonsense," replied the Duke. "For one moment at least you brought hope to our decimated forces! It gladdened our hearts to see the enemy in confusion and falling before the Venetians—even if it was only for a few minutes that we held the upper hand. And to see you and your valiant men fight completely through the entirety of the enemy ranks was a marvelous thing!"

"Nonetheless," replied D'Artagnan, "our efforts do not change the fact that Mantua will soon fall."

"Perhaps not," replied the Duke of Nevers, "but it has raised doubt in the minds of the Duke of Guantalla that he will easily be able to take the walls. In fact, it has raised enough doubt that he has sent an envoy to parley with us. Maybe, if we hold our cards hidden, we can bluff our way into preserving our lives."

D'Artagnan raised his disconsolate features. "The Duke of Guantalla desires to parley?"

"Yes," said the Duke of Nevers, "and I should like you to do the negotiating. In bringing the Count DeLucca to our aid you have amply demonstrated that you are a master at bluffing."

The crafty D'Artagnan considered this. "Then bring the envoy into your presence, but first line the streets along which he will pass with every soldier, even if you must pull them momentarily from the walls. We must make it look as though there is still ample strength within Mantua, and give the impression it will be very costly if they persist in taking the city."

The Duke of Nevers snapped his fingers and ordered his lieutenants to make it so.

"But," protested one of the lieutenants, "we can't leave our walls undefended!"

"Put helmets on women and children and place them temporarily on the walls so that they can pose as soldiers," said D'Artagnan. "Mantua is lost anyhow, this bluff may be our only chance of preserving the lives of the Duke and Duchess."

The envoy from Duke Guantalla was ushered through streets swarming with soldiery, so that it appeared there were many thousands of troops still defending Mantua. When the envoy was finally ushered into a tent with D'Artagnan and the Duke of Nevers, the musketeer's mouth dropped open in astonishment—for he recognized the Spanish outrider whose life he had spared.

"Why, my good friend D'Artagnan," said Juan Escarra. "You seemed surprised to see me."

D'Artagnan observed the bandage upon Escarra's shoulder, showing from beneath the uniform which was many ranks higher than the one the Spaniard had been wearing when he had been an outrider who fell into the musketeer's ambush. "I am surprised to see you—and that you seem to have been elevated in rank since we met not long ago. A meteoric rise it seems."

"Not so meteoric as it might appear," admitted Escarra. "I find it unnecessarily risky for me to wear my dress uniform when surveying the lay of the land. "It might make me a target for ambush and ransom."

"I believe you did not tell me the truth when you told me you would not be worth ransoming," chided D'Artagnan.

"Aah," replied Escarra. "That is not what I said. What I did say is that I am but a humble man with only enough means to purchase the horse I ride

"You seem surprised to see me."

upon and the weapons with which I serve my king—which is true enough."

"Well, nevertheless," said D'Artagnan with an artful shrug, "I am pleased to see that you have survived your wound and are actively engaged in the service of your country. Does your wound trouble you much?"

"It is stiff in the morning and at the end of the day, but if I do not overly exercise it there is no pain during the afternoon."

"That is good to hear," said D'Artagnan. "Let me introduce you to the Duke of Nevers."

The Duke of Nevers nodded stiffly to Escarra. "It seems you and D'Artagnan are acquainted?"

"First I became acquainted with a ball of lead cast from his musket," said Escarra. "D'Artagnan, himself, however, was much more pleasant."

The Duke of Nevers scowled.

Escarra read the expression and dismissed his own soldiers and attendants so that there were only he, D'Artagnan and the Duke of Nevers remaining. "Duke, you fear that I hold a grudge against D'Artagnan and will not deal leniently with you."

"That had occurred to me," said the Duke, "but let me assure we are prepared to fight to the last man. If you manage victory it will be costly!"

"Are you also prepared to fight to the last woman and child?" asked Escarra, "because that is whom I espied upon your walls with my field glass before I entered the city. I suspect your forces are not as numerous as your soldier crowded streets might suggest."

D'Artagnan chewed on the inside of his cheek, chagrined that his bluff had been called.

"Let me first tell you what the Duke Johann Von Aldringen has told me to procure—an unconditional surrender in which you, your family, and all of Mantua will be utterly at the mercy of his troops. And let me tell you his Hapsburg troops have a well-founded reput…"

"I am well aware of the reputation of the Hapsburg troops," snapped the Duke of Nevers. "I will tell you right now, I would rather fight to the death than unconditionally surrender."

"Precisely what I told the Duke Von Aldringen," said Escarra. "I told him you had nothing to gain by an unconditional surrender and that you would prefer to die in Mantua. Unfortunately, Von Aldringen found that option acceptable as well."

"Taking Mantua will be an expensive proposition," said D'Artagnan. "It will cost many Spanish and Hapsburg soldiers' lives."

"I do not want to see the blood of my fellow Spaniards spilled," said Escarra, "though in truth I do not concern myself so much if Hapsburg blood is lost. Still, I made an oath to D'Artagnan when he spared my life. I swore that I would someday return the favor, and I believe that today is that day."

"It was not as long in coming as I thought," admitted D'Artagnan. "What do you propose?"

"I propose that I persuade Duke Von Aldringen to let fifty people leave Mantua unmolested when you surrender the city. The lives of your soldiers will be spared."

"Done!" snapped the Duke of Nevers, who saw a way out of the horrible dilemma he had in many ways brought upon himself.

D'Artagnan frowned at how quickly the Duke of Nevers had accepted the proffered deal. "What, Duke? Perhaps we could have negotiated for more men to be released, or some other concessions had you not been so eager."

"I know a good deal when I hear it," replied the Duke of Nevers.

"It really is unlikely you shall receive a better offer than that," said Escarra. "In truth the only way I shall persuade Von Aldringen to accept this plan is by bringing to bear pressures from Don Gonzalo Fernandez de Cordoba, the Governor of Milan. His ribs still ache where they were kicked in by a giant riding a giant horse, and he is anxious to bring the war to an end. Also, when I propose the plan, I will say that you are demanding the release of 200 people, and this will give Von Aldringen some sense of victory when he is able to bargain you down to a mere 50 people who will be allowed to leave Mantua.

"The seven Venetians who fought all the way to the walls of Mantua with me must be include in those fifty," D'Artagnan told the Duke of Nevers."

"That will be difficult," hedged the Duke. "I have family and friends who will demand they be among the fifty."

"I shall not leave Mantua without them," said D'Artagnan.

"You shall not stay in Mantua," replied Escarra. "I could not guarantee your safety from the Count Von Aldringen. He is particularly angry at how you made him look a fool by cutting all the way through his lines."

"Surely, he must be mollified somewhat by the fact he managed to drive off the majority of the Venetian army," suggested D'Artagnan.

Escarra shook his head. "Very little, my French amigo. He feels that whole attack was merely a feint so that you could reach the walls of Mantua. Me...I suspect the Venetians were merely poorly organized and that was why they were so quickly routed."

"You may be closer to the truth," admitted D'Artagnan. "Still, General DeLucca is a prideful man. His ego may have been wounded enough that he will return with his troops for another engagement."

"He is also a cowardly and greedy man," said Escarra. "It baffles me how you convinced him to come against us in the first place, especially considering the high price we paid him in jewels and gold."

D'Artagnan offered Escarra an enigmatic smile, but not an explanation. "You are not the only one who can be persuasive, mon ami."

"Hah! D'Artagnan, why do you hesitate to share your secrets with me? Nevertheless, I think we have come to an accord. Let us eat and drink and bide our time telling stories, and then I shall go back to my encampment late in the day and tell them lies about my hard won negotiation, how you would prefer to die on the end of the sword, and how it was only with great persuasion I managed to convince you to accept my terms."

"And the seven Venetians?" questioned D'Artagnan.

"Perhaps I shall start your demands at 232 and work down to 58," said Escarra.

They passed the day telling many stories. That night another 96 within the walls of Mantua died from the plague. When Escarra returned, two hours after dawn, his news was mixed. Count Von Aldringen has agreed to fifty, and might have agreed to 58, if he had not discovered those extra eight would include D'Artagnan and his small band of Venetians.

"So I will stay in Mantua," resolved D'Artagnan.

"Not so quickly, amigo," replied Escarra. "I will assign the people who count the party leaving Mantua. I will instruct them that 58 is to be reported as 50—and thus you and your Venetians will be able to leave the city unmolested."

Already, the Count of Nevers had quietly chosen his retinue of 50 and they had packed every earthly possession they could possibly jam into a train of wagons, which departed the plague ridden streets of Mantua before the sun reached its apex over the Italian mountain ranges. The citizens cried out in anguish, for when they saw the Duke departing they knew all hope was lost.

Women scuttled into the street and threw themselves at the feet of Count Never's armed guard, begging to be taken along, offering their servitude and sometimes more if they should be accepted. The soldiers turned a deaf ear and a blind eye to these entreaties. D'Artagnan cursed his inability to save these poor wretches from the Hapsburg troops which would soon be rampaging through the city, looting the buildings and falling upon the women.

An undernourished woman who might have been a beauty when she was fully fed came up and thrust a toddler into D'Artagnan's arms. "Take Sebastian to his uncle Mateo Perez in Ferarra, I beg of you!"

D'Artagnan should have thrust the child back at his mother, but instead he put the dazed boy in the back of a cart and threw a blanket over him.

For long and tense minutes they waited while Spanish troops counted the Duke of Nevers departing retinue. "Fifty," agreed the three Spaniards, though they had clearly counted higher and all three had discovered the hidden child. Then the forlorn refugees departed the stench of the embattled city, driving their overburdened carts through enemy lines, listening to the mocking jeers of the soldiers, or seeing the relief on the faces of others as they realized these refugees signaled the war was coming to a close.

As they passed beyond the enemy lines a Spanish messenger came running up to D'Artagnan, pressed a note into his hand and then departed as quickly as he had arrived. Curious just what this message might be, D'Artagnan cut the anonymous wax seal with his thumbnail, opened the parchment, and read the message inscribed in French.

It has come to my attention that a certain individual from the Hapsburg camp has discovered your departure and is planning an attack upon your caravan in the guise of bandits so that the Hapsburg forces cannot be blamed for violating our agreement, should the matter come before the Pope. Be wary and be safe.

The note was unsigned, but D'Artagnan suspected it came from Escarra, for he was the only friend the musketeer had in the enemy camp. Likewise, he couldn't think of any reason why someone would send him such a note if it were not true.

D'Artagnan passed the warning onto the band of Venetian soldiers who began to load and prime a supply of extra muskets, removed from the Duke of Nevers" armory prior to their departure, they carried in the back of one of the carts.

The daughter-in-Law of the Duke of Nevers, Maria Gonzaga Nevers, comforted the crying Sebastian as the wagon lurched over the pot-holed roads. In fact, Maria was one of the Duke of Nevers' best claims to the duchies of Mantua and Monferrato, because she was the daughter of a more direct line of claim on Monferrato than either the Duke of Nevers or the Duke of Guantalla. This was something Pope Urban might take into consideration should they ever be able to take their case to arbitration before His Holiness.

Still, such a matter might never come to the consideration of the Pope if a a group of Hapsburg soldiers masquerading as bandits fell upon and killed them before they could reach the safety of the Papal State of Ferrara.

D'Artagnan made his way forward in the caravan, warning the soldiers to be wary and then reported the anonymous message to the Duke of Nevers, who for a moment lost his composure when the Duchess, having overheard the report, began to upbraid him for having ever abandoned Mantua in the first place.

"Silence, woman!" snapped the Duke. "We were doomed if we stayed in Mantua! If the plague didn't slay us the Hapsburg soldiers would have—if the Spanish were kind enough to spare our lives, that is."

"And now we are traipsing through the countryside like gypsies, only to be attacked by marauders!" exclaimed the Duchess. "We must go back to Mantua immediately!"

"That way is closed to us, Duchess," said D'Artagnan, when for a moment it appeared as though the Duke might actually be considering turning the caravan around. "We would be driven off or slain. I feel it is our best chance to keep moving forward with all possible speed to the shelter of Ferrara and be vigilant against attack."

"We were forced to leave behind many of our personal soldiers," lamented the Duke. "We have but twenty to fight against however many of Count Von Aldringen's rapacious Hapsburg soldiers he sends against us."

D'Artagnan sought to bolster the courage of the Duke and Duchess of Nevers, speaking with bravado beyond what he actually felt. "You also have seven of the best warriors of Venice—men who fought completely through both an army of Hapsburg soldiers and an army of Spanish soldiers. These will be able to hold off ten times their number—and if dare set aside my humility for a moment, you have D'Artagnan of the King Louis' musketeers. I may be worth ten or twenty men myself!"

No attack came upon the first or even the second day. On the third day, just when they had hope they might see the walls of Ferarra over the next hill or rise, a band of forty horsemen emerged from a copse of trees and moved to block the roadway. They were illy disguised, wearing ragged shirts over their Hapsburg uniforms, so it appeared they were bandits. However, few bandits had horses and weapons of such quality.

D'Artagnan heard the sound of hoof falls behind, and saw that their retreat was cut off as well by a score of men who were on foot.

"There's fewer men behind us!" urged the Duchess. "We can turn the caravan around and break through them!"

"An excellent strategy!" commended D'Artagnan, "if the men in the rear were the ones who were on the horses and we could slay them all as we broke through. However, the horsemen in front of us will run us down long before we are able to break through. Our carts make us very slow."

"Then put me on our swiftest horse," ordered the Duchess, "and I shall outrun them!"

"Our horses are tired and theirs appear fresh," replied the Duke. "They would capture you and you could not expect kind treatment from Hapsburg soldiers."

The Duchess sobered as she realized just what sort of depredations she could expect if she were captured.

"Our best chance is to keep our perimeter and see if we can drive them off," advised D'Artagnan. "There's only a few muskets between them, and I think we can even the odds before they reach us."

A man with a silver tooth that gleamed in a gleed of afternoon sunlight slipping through the overhead canopy of leaves, rode forward a few paces and called out to them in Italian, though the Austrian accent was discernible .

"Throw down your weapons and surrender. We'll take your goods and leave you unharmed!"

The Duchess laid her hand on her husband's arm. "Maybe we should listen to them!"

"They aren't actually bandits," the Duke of Nevers reminded her. "They are Hapsburg soldiers sent to exterminate us. If they can fool us into surrendering they'll be able to kill us all without losing a drop of their own blood."

"You have ten seconds to comply!" shouted the man with the silver tooth.

D'Artagnan threw the butt of his musket to his shoulder and sent a ball hurtling toward the leader. It was long range for a musket, which wasn't particularly accurate, but a combination of skill and luck sent the bullet through the fellow's chest. The false bandit lurched in his saddle, then slipped into the dust of the trail, where he lay convulsing.

Seeing they weren't going to have an uncontested victory, the Hapsburg bandits blocking the forward road charged toward the caravan. They galloped in a frightening cavalry charge, and D'Artagnan let them come. When the charge was thirty yards away he gave the order to fire and twenty muskets barked in unison, throwing up prodigious clouds of smoke and a screen of lead, which brought down four horses and seven bandits.

Horses shrieked as they were trampled, and other horses stumbled and fell, throwing riders. For long moments there was a horrible chaos of flailing hooves, crushed men, and broken equines and the charge was momentarily stopped.

As D'Artagnan had instructed them, the non-combatant members of the caravan handed up loaded muskets and so his soldiers were able to deliver another deadly volley into the shambolic mass of horse flesh and humans.

Now D'Artagnan heard a second volley delivered from the rear of the caravan, but the false bandits who had muskets or pistols were returning fire now, and one of the Duke's French soldiers, sank suddenly to the earth as a ball burrowed into his brain.

Bullets ripped at the carts, casting up splinters and cutting through tarps. Sebastian and the other children of the caravan screamed in terror. The surviving bandit horsemen who were not tangled and mired in the fallen front ranks drew back and streamed around the edges of the morass of dead and dying.

In moments they would be upon the caravan and the fighting would be hand to hand. D'Artagnan drew one pistol after the other and loosed succeeding shots which managed to take down one of the horsemen. He drew his sword and as he raised it in what would likely be a futile attempt to defend himself against a mounted cavalry rider, the clarion sound of a horn cut through the din and he heard a great bellowing roar that indicated the arrival of fresh combatants—but from what quarter and persuasion D'Artagnan could not say.

Neither could the Hapsburg troops masquerading as bandits know who these fresh arrivals might be, and given the heavy casualties that had just been inflicted upon them, they turned their horses and bolted into the thick of the forest. Likewise, the charging mob at the rear of the caravan melted into the woods, leaving behind seven or eight bodies to carpet the roadway.

D'Artagnan had no time to be relieved, for the newcomers might just as easily be foes as friends. "Reload your muskets!" he ordered the soldiers of the caravan.

Before they could complete the task, three mounted figures came into view over the rise in the trail. Two of these were elegant figures, resplendent in the uniform of the French musketeer, and the third was an enormous figure mounted on an equally enormous steed.

D'Artagnan's heart leaped for he recognized these as his fast friends and fellow musketeers from whom he had been parted months before.

As they drew nearer, Athos again winded his horn, and Porthos let out a prodigious bellow which sounded as loud as twenty or thirty men.

"Hah!" laughed Aramis as they drew near to the caravan. "Our ruse seems to have frightened your craven attackers." Beneath the hooves of his horse one fallen bandit attempted to draw his sword and rise. Aramis fired his pistol into the unfortunate man's body, so that he sagged back to the earth.

D'Artagnan gave the order and the caravan's soldiers rushed forth to dispatch any surviving bandits.

"It is a curious thing," commented Athos, after giving another long blast on his horn, "that these bandits appear to be wearing the Hapsburg uniform beneath their rags."

"You are a sight for my beleaguered eyes!" exclaimed D'Artagnan. "What brings you to me, my friends?!"

"Why, we heard you were having some troubles—beyond your usual complications with women," bellowed Porthos. "However, the king was reluctant to let us out of his service—and finally we had to make an excuse for a short absence and rode, as fast as our horses would allow, to reach you in Mantua."

"Where we learned from a fellow named Escarra that you had left a day and a half before," continued Athos.

"And how fares Mantua?" questioned the Duchess.

Athos swept off his hat in deference to the Duchess. "It goes ill for the residents of Mantua, I fear. Count Von Aldringen has given his troops leave to loot the city, and the survivors of Mantua tremble in fear of their depredations."

Porthos cantered his horse forward to lay a heavy hoof on the chest of a stunned bandit who had finally regained enough of his senses to draw out a reserve pistol. Once the weight of the horse, and the musketeer riding it, settled on the bandit's chest, he gave a final gasp and loosed the pistol.

"These bandits are of a weak constitution I fear," said Porthos, mournfully. "Perhaps you did not really need our assistance, D'Artagnan."

"Nonsense," replied D'Artagnan. "There were many of them and I always welcome the aid and the jovial company of the doughty Porthos to lift my spirits—for these have been grim days."

"Yes," replied Aramis. "We have seen the heavy hand of the plague on the land."

After they had dispatched the remaining Hapsburg bandits, saving one with a loose tongue who was able to speak Italian fluently and offered to testify in the Papal courts to the intrigue which the Count Von Aldringen had been involved, they continued on their way to Ferarra, short just one slain and with two injured from their encounter.

When D'Artagnan finished relating his escapades in Monferrato to Aramis he paused. "I can't help but think that maybe there was some real power to the sacrificial rites the false Countess Bianchi was performing to Resheph beneath the church, and that I am somehow responsible for the plague that has come upon the land."

"Why would you even burden yourself with such thoughts?" replied Aramis. "And why speak them to me?"

"Because you are a devout man," replied D'Artagnan, "who may one day be a man of the cloth...and there is no other man of the cloth among us, so I must unburden my soul to you."

"Very well," decided Aramis. "I shall be your confessor—but still I am not convinced there is a sin to confess, aside from your flagrant disregard of the sanctity of marriage, a serious enough sin, but one which is certainly a common enough affliction."

"It is something that Martina said," replied D'Artagnan. "She told me that she was sacrificing her own flesh and blood to Resheph."

"Of course she was referring to her sister, but you stopped that when you interrupted their rites," objected Aramis.

"I did," agreed D'Artagnan, "but when Martina threw herself at me with upraised knife she died upon the point of my sword and she fell up the altar of Resheph...her blood staining the altar."

"The same altar where she intended to sacrifice her sister," concluded Aramis.

"The same," agreed D'Artagnan.

"So, because she literally, though accidentally, sacrificed herself upon the altar of this so-called god of plague, you feel that the curse was called forth upon the land?"

"The evidence is written in the corpses piled in the streets of Mantua," said D'Artagnan.

"Such heavy thoughts do not become you, my friend," replied Aramis. "Now, for the sake of argument, let us say that this Resheph is indeed an incarnation of Satan's power, which is able to bring down a plague upon the land by a blood sacrifice."

"Yes?" questioned D'Artagnan.

"You were in the crypt that night to stop the sacrifice of Ludovica, were you not?" questioned Aramis.

"I was," agreed D'Artagnan whole-heartedly."

"And you succeeded in that aim, did you not?"

"I did," replied D'Artagnan, "but in doing so I inadvertently shed the blood of Martina upon that Satanic alt…"

"Stop there," replied Aramis. "You had no malicious intention or evil desires. If indeed this plague is a curse brought about by Resheph or even Satan it is on the head of Martina and her followers, not upon yours. If they had not reared that altar and spoken the incantations none of this should ever have come about."

"I suppose that is true," agreed D'Artagnan reluctantly.

"You should not suppose that it is true, for it is an indisputable fact!" replied Aramis, "so even without priestly vestments I am able to absolve you of that sin, which was no sin at all."

"I do feel as though a burden has been lifted," reported D'Artagnan.

"Trouble yourself with it no more," replied Aramis. "However, as for your indiscretions with the false Countess Bianchi—those you should resolve with a real priest…perhaps when we reach Ferarra."

"I shall do so," said D'Artagnan.

"Is there any other affliction which is burdening your soul?" inquired Aramis.

"Just a pair of tasks which I must accomplish; namely, delivering young Sebastian to his aunt and uncle, and a visit to Milan to break off an engagement which I never made."

"Oh ho!" replied Aramis. "That is a tale I should like to hear."

"And I will tell it over a cup or two of wine," replied D'Artagnan, "when we reach Ferarra." He paused for a moment. "Dare I ask if Queen Anne has mentioned me in my absence?"

"She was greatly sorrowful at first," answered Aramis, "however, I am pleased to announce she has found another favorite and has discovered solace in his arms…and bed, if the tales are true."

"How is that good news?!" cried a pained D'Artagnan.

"It is good news because King Louis no longer harbors suspicions against you—and will soon recall you to Paris. It is good news because he has no longer condemned you to die in foreign lands. Perhaps, you will soon be doing your duty protecting the king on French soil!"

"I suppose I cannot fault the Queen for finding solace in another's arms, when I did the same," replied D'Artagnan finally. He sighed.

"You cannot fault Queen Anne for anything she does," answered Aramis. "She is the queen, after all!"

Finis

Writing the Devil of Monferrato

Just prior to the opportunity to write The Devil of Monferrato, I'd recently completed reading the entirety of Alexandre Dumas' musketeer saga so, hopefully, this aided me in capturing the voices and personalities of the infamous four musketeers.

Though there have been a number of incarnations and interpretations in writing and in film of Dumas' most memorable characters, I chose to draw my inspiration from the original prose. I freely admit, however, that my interpretations of Athos, Aramis, Porthos, and D'Artagnan are no more valid than any other literary upstart riding on Dumas' coattails.

In fact, my interpretations may be tainted by the whiff of the supernatural, the addition of which the reader may or may not find agreeable. But I couldn't help myself, considering I have written one other musketeer story before, and it was a variation on the musketeer's famous taking of the Bastions of Saint Gervais, but in addition to Rochellais enemies the four musketeers find and defeat some Cthulhuesque monstrosities. However, it was my research of France's Italian wars and politics during the time of the musketeers that led me to write the story I did. The motivations and genealogies are muddied and complicated, but I did my best to sort them out or, rather, I tossed the musketeers in the middle of that political mire and let them do their best to sort them out—with the same sort of mixed and, hopefully, entertaining results they experience in the Dumas tales.

JOEL JENKINS - lives in the heron-haunted shadows of the Rainier Mountains, and finds the perpetual twilight conducive to writing. He is the former front-man for several obscure rock bands, was once nearly shot by the law, and impersonated a ghost on a number of occasions.

He is best known for his sword and science fiction Dire Planet series and currently has over forty novels and collections in print.

The Lady of Acadia

by Paul Beale

The sounds are all too familiar to a man like this. That sound of the horses' hooves against the dry ground. The crack of the whip and the creak of the stage coach wheels as the carriage navigates a hard turn at high speed. They are sounds every highwayman can recognize long before the coach is in sight. He hides behind some trees as the coachman drives his team past, just as planned. Once they are out of site he urges his black steed across the road and up the hill on the other side.

"Heyaaa!" he yells as he digs his heels into the horse's side, confident that the stagecoach is too far away to hear his prompt.

The hill is steep but little trouble for the large horse. Once at the top the Highwayman lights the lantern he is carrying with a match and waves it furiously. Only seconds later he spies the answer he was expecting. Another signal light from a nearby hill tells him that his compatriots are in place. Snuffing out the light and tossing it aside he once again springs into a gallop. Feeling the confidence that comes with the kind of success he and his band have enjoyed in recent weeks, he smiles. If he bothered to look back behind him his confidence would fade quickly. Now trotting into the same clearing at the top of the hill where he had just been, another rider appears. Unlike the dark rider who had just occupied this vantage point, this rider is a man of light. He is dressed in a blue and white uniform with an unmistakable crest on his chest. It is the symbol of the King's Musketeers. He pauses only for a moment before following. He too allows himself a confident smile but his is based on what he knows is coming.

A half mile away the coach continues its ride toward fate. On top of the coach is an older coachman, or so it seems. Inside a somewhat overweight female passenger and across from her a man with a cane that hints at injury, or so it seems.

Bang! Cracks the musket of a gun, startling both the horses and the coaches' occupants as the coachman pulls back on the reins.

"Highwaymen!" warns the coachman.

"Stand and deliver," orders the lead horseman as he and three others

86

surround the carriage. "Everyone out now," he continues, "Move!"

Taken by surprise there is nothing the coachman can do but put his arms up in the air. The two passengers appear just as helpless as they exit the coach.

"Oh dear this is terrible," shrieks the middle aged lady as she stumbles to the road, a fan partially covering her face.

"Now, now Madame I'm sure we will be okay," encourages the other passenger as he carefully departs the coach, careful not to fall over on his bad leg.

"You'll be just fine Mademoiselle as long as you cooperate," assures the leader of the bandits. "All we want are your valuables."

"I suspect that's all anyone ever wanted from her," jokes a second robber as he and his partners burst into laughter.

"Well I never," protests the damsel.

"I'll bet you haven't," the leader quips with a smile, "Now if you could just place your valuables in this bag we can make this quick. Oh and driver, my friend here will be taking that strong box," he says as he motions to a metal crate behind the driver.

"A friend comes," is the call heard by all as the last of the highwaymen rides into the scene.

His dark horse is a startling site as it comes to a sudden stop. This is the same man from the top of the hill. As planned he has joined his crew to finish off the nights work. He is greeted with smiles but few words.

"A friend comes," is the call that comes again but this time surprise is what greets the call.

"What? We have no more friends in these woods," the leader announces.

"He's not calling to you," the coachman says with a wide grin just before he throws the strong box at the group's leader.

"Aaah," yells the leaders as the box knocks him from his horse.

"To arms, we are attacked," blurts out the dark rider as he sees the form of a young Musketeer riding into the scene.

With his wheelock pistol in one hand and his rapier in the other D'artagnan controls his white stallion with his reins in his mouth. Firing a shot into the shoulder of the mounted dark rider first, D'artagnan follows that volley by crashing into two of the others knocking them from their horses. They struggle to their feet and turn toward both D'artagnan and the coach passengers. Gone however the old man and plumb woman are. Instead the thieves see two more Musketeers. The grey wig worn by Aramis has been discarded to reveal his dark flowing hair. The cane that held him up is now pulled apart to reveal one half is a long blade. Next to him is the often jovial Porthos who tries valiantly to look series in his frilly dress. Without the fan his beard is more than noticeable but it's the pistol he pulls from his purse that catches the criminals' eyes. Adding to their trouble is the realization that the coachman is part of the ruse. Athos has also pulled a pistol and is aiming at their leader.

"If you could be so kind as to drop your weapons, gentlemen," request the smiling Musketeer.

Surprised and shaken by the turn of events, the four men briefly look at each other as if to look for someone to present a solution to their predicament. All are too stunned however and the four Musketeers have the drop on them. With a sigh the leader drops his weapon and puts his hands up. His comrades follow suit quickly.

"A wise move my good people, the beautiful Lady Porthos is a dead shot," quips Athos laughing.

"Very funny, next time you can wear the dress," fires back Porthos. "I don't understand why we needed a fake female passenger," he continues.

"We didn't," D'artagnan explains, "We just thought it would be a good laugh".

"What?" shouts Porthos, as his friends break into laughter.

By the time the four King's Musketeers have returned to Paris with their prisoners in tow, Porthos is almost over being angry with his mates, almost. The once glamorous gentlemen bandits are no less angry. Tied by the hands they are lead on foot behind the mounted Musketeers. Their exploits have made them folk heroes to the frustration of the King, so Athos insists on making a show of their capture. It seems to have achieved the desired effect. The scattered cheers are all for the popular Musketeers.

The leader of the thieves protests the public humiliation. "Could you not have found a less crowded path to take us?" he asked.

"Why I thought you would prefer the view better this way. Besides you should enjoy the sunlight while you can. The Bastille is somewhat gloomy" Athos points out.

The highwaymen's embarrassing journey ends shortly as the proud friends lead them through a short alley into a courtyard at Musketeer headquarters. They are greeted with cheers from their fellow members of the King's guard.

"Bravo! Lieutenant you have captured the robbers who have been terrorizing the roads around Paris," announces one Musketeer.

D'artagnan's promotion to lieutenant is recent enough that for a moment he does not realize the old Musketeer is talking to him. Once he does a smile comes across his face.

"We have captured them my good man," he says motioning to his friends. "Could you be so kind as to deliver these four to the proper authorities?"

"Gladly D'artagnan and good job, all of you," answers the veteran Musketeer.

The capture of the bandits is a feather in the cap of the entire Musketeer core. The Cardinal's Guardsmen were also dispatched to detain the bandits. The fact that the Musketeers have again bested them brings prestige to the King's finest. That prestige as always is shared by all. After all their moto is "all for one and one for all." None will enjoy the boost more however than their leader, Captain de Tre'ville. As good fortune would have it the Captain has witnessed their arrival.

"D'artagnan could you and your troop join me in my office please?" asks a voice from a nearby window.

"Of course Captain, right away," comes the reply.

Older than the Three Musketeers, even Athos but still in good enough shape to wield his rapier, Tre'ville commands the respect of all who serve under him. On this day he looks more serious than usual despite the success of their mission.

"Is everything all right, sir?" questions Athos.

"WH... oh yes of course Athos, I'm just a bit preoccupied. You did a fine job with the highwaymen case," he replies

"Thank you sir," says Athos with a curious look on his face. He is not used to seeing the Captain this way.

"Gentlemen I must confess I am indeed concerned about something. May I speak to you in confidence," he asks?

"Of course sir, we will not speak a word to anyone," assures D'artagnan.

"I know you will not. You are a fine group of Musketeers and on many occasions have proven your loyalty. The matter I wish to discuss is not official Musketeer business as it involves the Cardinal," Tev'ville explains.

"Doesn't it always," quips Porthos.

"We have run afoul of Cardinal Richelieu to many times of late and even I am on thin ice but let me explain. Are any of you familiar with Charles de Saint – Etienne de Latour?" says Tre'ville.

"Yes of course, he's the governor of Acadia. I met him once a long time ago," declares Athos.

"Well unfortunately he and his position are being contested by one of the Cardinal's allies, Charles De Menou d'Aulnay. Both Latour and d'Aulnay were awarded land in the New World that partly overlaps. Recently d'Aulnay's forces raided a trading post a day's ride from Latour's main base of operations, Fort Latour. He dispatched his wife Madame Latour to return to France to rally support among their friends and bring back men and arms to defend their lands on the northern shore of the Bay of Fundy."

"I take it Cardinal is not one of their friends," interrupts Aramis.

"Indeed he is not. Richelieu is the one who placed d'Aulnay in his position. He has a vested interest in seeing the Latours pushed from the New World and his man d'Aulnay in control."

"And the King? What is his role in this affair?" questions Athos.

"The King is preoccupied and kept in the dark by Richelieu. His majesty has far too much trust for the Cardinal," responds Tre'ville.

"Then the Lady Latour…," starts D'artagnan.

"Is walking into a trap almost as soon as she reaches French soil I'm afraid. Antoine de Laval has been dispatched by Richelieu to make sure the Lady does not survive to meet with her allies. He is a minor but ambitious and ruthless member of the court. There are also rumors that Bon Varlet may be involved," continues Tre'ville.

The mention of Bon Varlet makes the hair stand up on the Musketeers' necks. His reputation as "The Musketeer Killer" precedes him where ever he goes.

"I am far too familiar with Laval. We have had a, shall we say run in recently and Bon Varlet, well you know about him," says Athos.

"I have heard, oh don't look so surprised. There is little that goes on in Paris that I am not aware of. I am not concerned with your little scuffle with Laval. At any rate Charles is an old friend of mine and I do not wish to see any harm come to his young wife. Unfortunately I have received explicate orders not to involve myself in any way in the affairs of New France. It has been declared out of the Musketeer's jurisdiction. I am powerless to render aid in any official capacity," laments the Captain.

"Indeed, well that is most unfortunate. I am glad however that you summoned us to your office. You see the four of us were hoping we could have a leave," remarks Athos with a smile.

"We were?" ask a confused Porthos before he is elbowed by Aramis. "Uh…ah yes that is we were," he recovers.

"Indeed, I thought you might need a rest after your recent adventure," smiles their leader. "I have little choice but to grant your request what with the way I have been over working you four," Tre'ville continues with a glint in his eye and a pen in his hand ready to draw up their leave.

"Very kind of you sir, perhaps we will head to the coast," announces D'artagnan as he looks at the Captain for a reaction.

"I hear Auray is nice this time of year," directs Tre'ville.

"I have heard the same. Auray it is then," concludes D'artagnan.

Indeed the conversation is nearly complete as the five men have said all they need to say without really saying anything, officially.

"Well gentlemen, enjoy your much deserved leave. I trust it will be interesting," says Tre'ville as he stands to shake their hands one by one.

"Thank you sir and don't worry about the other matter. I'm sure the good Lord will provide a solution," encourages Aramis.

Of course everyone in the room knows that they have been dancing around that solution as Auray is where Lady Latour is to land. As they leave the office of the Captain of the Musketeers they stop at the desk of his assistant.

"The Captain would like you to forward us our pay early as we are on leave as of today," Aramis announces.

"Make sure they get the reward for the capture of the highwaymen as well," reminds a loud voice from Tre'ville's office.

"Yes Captain," responds the young female assistant as the four adventurers smile.

"Thank you my dear and what pray tell is your name?" ask Aramis as he leans in toward her.

"Aramis come on. We have no time for your romancing," barks Athos as the other two laugh.

"Another time my dear," Aramis finishes as he kisses her hand as she smiles.

Hours later the people of the French countryside, outside Paris, view a site that instills confidence and pride. Four Musketeers on horseback in full stride, their insignia crested vest flowing in the wind. Most striking is the lead rider D'artagnan on his tall white steed. The journey to Auray will take far too long for their liking and they will have to change horses at this pace. Fortunately Aramis has friends along their path who will lend them mounts and take care of their animals.

Lodging in Auray is sparse but a King's Musketeer can always find aid. Once in their room above a local tavern three of the four friends meet to rest and plan.

"The lady's ship is just off shore, why have they not docked?" asks Porthos.

"Athos is inquiring around discreetly, I'm sure he will find out," answers D'artagnan.

"I believe that's him now," remarks Porthos as all three hear someone coming up the creaky old stairs. A knock on the door is answered quickly by the eager trio.

"Athos, what have you found out?" blurts out Porthos.

"I've learned much my friends. The lady Latour is already ashore but is in hiding. She was warned in time of Richelieu's plotting. Her and a small party came ashore last night in a small launch but have been unable to return to the ship or make it out of the town."

"Curse Richelieu and his malicious agents. How many are we up against?" queries D'artagnan.

"From what I can gather there may be as much as twelve of the Cardinal's Guards in Auray led by Laval but they are not wearing their uniforms. Even with that they are not hard to spot. I have spied four so far myself. No sign of Bon Varlet yet," replies Athos.

"Ha, twelve of the Cardinal's toy soldiers. Not enough to work up a sweat," boasts Porthos.

"Perhaps but it takes only one to harm the Lady we came here to protect. We will have to act quickly and with stealth. First we must change our attire. We are after all supposed on vacation and not on official Musketeers business." says Athos.

"Indeed but where will we find her?" Ask Aramis.

"I have already acquired that information. Richelieu has few friends in this little port town. The Lady Latour is on the edge of town hidden by a friend in a barn. She will not be safe there long. The Cardinal's vultures are growing restless and I fear will soon begin searching house to house. It grows dark now. In an hour we will make our way to her hiding place. For now we all need to change to our street clothes," finishes Athos.

An hour is always the same number of minutes but this one seems to go on forever. The edginess broken only by a few jokes aimed at Porthos and his flamboyant attire. While the others are dressed to be inconspicuous, Porthos had no such cloths in his wardrobe. The dandy gentleman will just have to make do.

Sixty minutes later the four heroes make their way down the stairs and out a back door to an alley. Having made the mistake of entering Auray in their Musketeer uniforms it is likely their adversaries are aware of their presence and are watching the tavern. Slinking into the shadows D'artagnan thinks is most un-musketeer like. More like the Cardinal's Guard or his many nefarious agents. Still, as much as he would relish another battle with those red vested snakes now is not the time. Captain

Tre'ville is not just their commanding officer but a trusted friend and ally. Strict as he may be, the good Captain has always had their back and this escapade gives them a chance to repay that loyalty. Few words are spoken as they peer around dark corners before darting to the next building. Hand signals replace their usual jovial banter. For Aramis the silence is excruciating as it robs him of a chance to take more verbal shots at Porthos's extravagant and in his mind ridiculous clothing. For the cause, he holds his tongue and laughter at the site of the ox-like dandy trying to sneak around among the houses and small back yard gardens. He does manage a head shake and grin when Porthos looks his way. The only reply possible from the plump adventurer is a confused look.

"There, there, that house by the end of the town," motions Athos.

But before they can undertake the last leg of their journey Athos puts his hand up to stop D'artagnan's advance.

"Wait, look," he warns as he points to four figures on the far side of the yard sneaking toward the house.

While dressed in everyday clothing all four know who they are. The Cardinal's minions are the only other people with business here.

"They are going for the house, good. Latour is in the barn. D'artagnan and I will fetch the Lady. You two dispose of the intruders," orders Athos.

"Thank Heavens! For a moment I was afraid you were going to suggest we fight them four on four. That would not have been very sporting," smiles Porthos as he bursts from the bushes.

"Indeed your attire should blind our enemies making this a short fight," quips Aramis, relieved to be able to return to badgering of his friend.

Quickly and purposely Aramis rushes past his comrade. As much as they may jostle with each other verbally they are the best of friends.

"You are just jealous of my sense of style," he claims as he meets and engages his first foe.

The Cardinal's Vipers shout out warnings and directions to each other but it is all background noise to the two Musketeers as they spring into action. Their banter seems to even overwhelm the sound of steel against steel and the grunts of their enemies.

"Oh yes that's it ha-ha, I have always wanted to dress like a clown," continues Aramis as his rapier claims its first victim with a stab to the heart.

In the background behind them the Guardsmen can see Athos and D'artagnan running to the barn but they are far too busy to care or wonder why. D'artagnan allows himself a quick look toward the skirmish as he makes his way hastily to the rear of the property. He smiles as he sees the inhumanly strong Porthos throwing an animal feeding troth at a surprised guardsman. D'artagnan is not surprised by this show of power however. He has seen Porthos perform too many feats of strength. He just smiles and continues to follow Athos to the barn. Had they not been in such a rush they might have thought better than to burst in unannounced.

"Look out!" yells Athos as he ducks, narrowly avoiding the sting of a dagger.

He looks at the knife stuck to the barn door briefly then turns to see its owner.

"Stand back! I'm warning you," barks the voice of a young boy.

Barely fourteen Pierre is brave beyond his years but no match for two fully armed men. Average in weight and height for his years he is notable only by his well-groomed red hair.

"Step aside Pierre I will handle these two. No Cardinal's men will ever take me," exclaims the beautiful young lady behind the teen as she moves ahead of her young protector.

"I will thank you not to insult us in that way Madame. We are not the Cardinal's men," replies an insulted Athos strongly.

"Then who are you? Take care how you answer. I am fully versed in the art of swordplay," warns Latour.

"I have no doubt you are my lady. We are here to aid you," explains D'artagnan as he holds his hands up to show he means no harm.

"Who sent you?" asks the lady in as gruff a tone as she can muster.

"Tre'ville my lady," answers Athos.

"Musketeers, you're Musketeers? Thank God," she exhales with relief.

"We are indeed but keep that too quiet. We are not here officially," says Athos.

"Then my allies have lost their bid to sway the King and recruit aid for my husband," bemoans the discouraged heroine.

Briefly the two Musketeers pause as the lady walks into the light. Her beauty is breathtaking and despite her small size she has an air of strength about her. Her dark hair and attire are both best described as practical for a woman on a dangerous mission. Even with that she makes her look seem feminine.

"I'm afraid so my Lady but at least we can insure that you are able to make it safely back to your ship," offers Athos once he catches his breath.

D'artagnan is much slower to recover from the stunning sight of the petit beauty and he quickly reminds himself that she is married, to a friend of Tre'ville's no less.

"*I am fully versed in the art of swordplay*"

"There is little time my Lady. Already four of the Cardinal's agents engage my men outside. We must leave immediately," Athos explains.

"Yes, if I cannot find help for my husband's efforts than I must return to be at his side," she says as she boldly pushes past the two surprised rescuers.

Pierre is clearly used to the speed and determination at which she moves and is right behind her. She strides down from a small embankment towards the house where she sees Aramis and Porthos standing over four dead men.

"This must be the Lady Latour," says Aramis as he bows in his best gallant form, waving his hat as he dips forward.

"The Cardinal's men I assume?" she replies looking down at the recently deceased bodies in front of her.

"That would be our guess as well but it seems we are all here in an unofficial capacity," remarks Porthos.

"I think it best if we make our way to the docks as soon as possible my Lady," advises Athos.

"Agreed, my men aboard the ship are waiting for a signal in case we cannot make our way inland. Sadly there are less of us returning to the ship. Allies of the men you dispatched of ambushed us in the town's center and killed two of my men. With your aid I am sure we can deal with the rest," Latour confidently says.

Without exception all those with her are amazed at both her confidence and her ability to take control. Even Athos the natural leader and D'artagnan the ranking Musketeer on this mission become quickly aware that she intends to be the one in charge. The four friends each decide on their own to defer to her plans until such time as they feel there is need to step in.

"What is the signal your ship is waiting for?" quarries D'artagnan.

"I'm to wave a torch from the docks. We had better do it soon before our enemies decide to attempt to board the ship," she adds as she begins to make her way to the waterfront.

They are careful but less stealthy than the Musketeers had been making their way to the barn. The numbers are more even now and while she would prefer to avoid more violence the odds are on her side now. Soon they are near the dockside.

"My Lady look," warns Pierre as he ducks behind a stone building and the others follow suit despite not knowing what he has seen.

"What is it? Is it the rest of the Cardinal's agents?" asks Porthos.

"Yes and I cannot get to where I need to in order to send the signal. If Tre'ville sent you four than I assume you can deal with them?" she says half asking and half stating.

"There are only nine of Laval's men; it shouldn't be a problem for my fellow Musketeers.

"I'll escort the Lady to the shore," orders a smiling D'artagnan as he peers around the corner. His smile is no act. The young adventurer relishes the danger perhaps even more than the others. His mostly successful attempt to be taken seriously as a leader cannot mask his swashbuckling ways.

"After you," Aramis motions to Porthos.

"Gladly" replies the plump swordsman.

Pistols in one hand and rapiers in the other, the three charge out into the street with purpose. There is no need for stealth now and the sound of gun fire breaks the relative silence with death following each blast. Three of their foes fall including Laval. His demise stuns and disrupts his men.

"All for one and one for all!" cry the three as they launch into their foes.

With first shots spent and no time to reload their single shot side arms they depend on the weapons that they are best known for, their swords. The six remaining jackals minus Laval do their best to regroup but the element of surprise has given the Musketeers an edge.

While they battle in the street D'artagnan leads his group to the dock and a mooring where Latour's row boat had been left but all they see is a half sunken launch.

"Sabotage," exclaims Pierre.

Unshaken he reaches for the torch that they had earlier hidden under the wharf. Taking a match he strikes it and lights the signal. Making his way to a place where he can be easily seen he waves the torch wildly. A quick response comes from the "Acadia" the flag ship of the Latour family's mostly far flung fleet. Unfortunately they are not the only ones who have seen the light show. Three previously hidden assailants burst from an ally and rush past the battle toward D'artagnan, Pierre and Francoise Latour.

"My Lady behind us!" warns the brave lieutenant as he draws his sword. "En garde" he says in the traditional fencing greeting.

Two of the men engage him and a third attacks the Lady who shows herself to be a capable swordswoman.

"Keep the torch up Pierre, we'll deal with these three," commands Latour.

"Yes my Lady," answers the loyal cabin boy as he waves the torch even harder.

From the ship comes a reply. A deck hand assigned to watch the dock continues to wave a lantern. It is a pre-arranged sign that the signal has been seen. On the "Acadia" the night watch burst into activity, waking all aboard and preparing to pull the anchor.

"They have seen us," announces Pierre.

"Good my friend, now a little help please?" asks Francoise who is having a little trouble fending off her particularly skilled attacker.

Pulling a knife from his ever present knife belt Pierre throws it forcefully at her adversary lodging it in his mid-section. He drops instantly.

"Thank you," she says quietly as she pauses briefly saddened by the lack of remorse in her young allies face.

He has had a hard life and the innocence of youth has long been gone from his life. There is no telling where he would be if the Latours had not taken him in. Francoise has no time to ponder about Pierre or anything else. She turns towards where D'artagnan was battling two men. She is relieved to see that he has already dispatched one and the other is clearly no match for him. In the background she sees the other Musketeers are winning as well. Pierre pulls another knife from the many hiding places in his clothes but Latour signals him to stop.

"He will not need your help Pierre," she says with a smile.

As if on cue, D'artagnan thrust his rapier into the villain's stomach. He turns quickly to access the situation, first to the Lady and then to his friends. Finally he looks to the "Acadia" where he sees a launch being lowered. The small boat that had carried her party to Auray had been destroyed by the Cardinal's men so the only way for her to her escape is a second boat. All seems to be going better than expected. For a moment D'artagnan wonders if escape is necessary but that hope only last for a few seconds. From the end of the long cobblestone street that lines the wharf he hears and then sees a mounted troop of assailants galloping their way, pistols in hand.

"Athos beware!" warns D'artagnan, hoping his friends would see the danger in time. They did but the Musketeers re out gunned and caught in a near defenceless position.

"We have them D'artagnan, get the Lady to safety," orders Athos in as confident a voice as he can muster.

D'artagnan is no fool and knows that by standing their ground his friends may be sacrificing their lives. He sees Aramis quickly pick up an unfired gun from a dead guardsman and fire it at the lead horseman. In the confusion of combat he manages a rare miss but the bullet strikes the rider behind his target. It is enough to make them pull up. A second shot fired from down the street by D'artagnan strikes another man in the arm. He had reloaded his pistol with a speed only a veteran soldier could equal.

"Nice shot Aramis," remarks Porthos.

"I was aiming for Bon Varlet," exclaims a frustrated Aramis.

The others had not even recognized Bon Varlet, or more accurately the Count De Bon Varlet. The name draws an immediate and harsh reaction on the faces of the three heroes. Bon Varlet is one of the Cardinal's agents and is known quietly among the king's Court as "The Musketeer Killer." The tall, dark haired Count with eyes even darker than his mane is fit for a forty year old and dangerous beyond equal. They duck into an alley to reload while Bon Varlet's Black Patrol also seeks cover. The Title of Black Patrol is well deserved. Numbering twelve before this night they are two less now and are not very happy about it.

"Athos, I smell your stench in this!" yells Bon Varlet.

"You will soon be doing more than smelling me Bon Varlet," replies Athos as he fires a shot just missing his nemesis.

The shot is answered by a volley of musket fire that rips off the small shop the Musketeers are hiding behind. Bon Varlet and Athos have a history. Bon Varlet is rumored to have killed a close friend and fellow Musketeer of his. Once again there was no proof. Unseen at first by all, two of Bon Varlet's nefarious crew have made their way silently toward the dock and are hidden behind several barrels and crates. As the row boat from the "Acadia" nears the dock two shots ring out killing the men in the tiny vessel. One slumps forward while the other falls into the harbour.

"No!" cries Francoise as she sees two of her loyal men slain.

"Get down!" shouts D'artagnan as he fires a shot, killing one of the bushwhackers.

The boat continues to drift toward the shore, close enough for Pierre to grab its bow. The other attacker reloads quickly but as he pops up to fire he is hit from the side. D'artagnan looks toward the alley to see Porthos wave and smile. D'artagnan returns the smile but it does not last long as his friend is suddenly hit by a blast that rips into his arm.

"Porthos!" yells D'artagnan.

"Go D'artagnan, get them out of here," commands Athos.

While torn D'artagnan has little choice. He knows the others will do whatever it takes to help the fallen Porthos. He also knows that he is the only one who can help Latour now. Determined and confident, he springs into action.

"Into the boat," he says directing the Lady and Pierre to their escape. Reluctantly they comply.

"I can row" says D'artagnan, take this and cover us," he says as he hands Francoise his loaded pistol.

She takes the gun as Pierre pushes the boat away from the dock. Heart sick at the prospect of leaving his friends, but determined to save the Lady Latour and Pierre, D'artagnan rows like a man possessed.

Back on shore all seems lost for our heroes but help is on the way. From the Acadia a blast from its cannon fires and rips into the section of the dock where the Cardinal's men have sought cover. Two more drop amid screams and confusion. The three Musketeers use the chaos to make their escape, helping Porthos all the way. Moving as quickly as they can into the livery stable they mount their unsaddled horses. Wounded but not wanting to slow his friends Porthos hurls himself onto his horse. Meanwhile Bon Varlet's Black Patrol has gathered their senses and have made their way to the stable. The three fighters are in no shape for another gun battle. Kicking the side of their mounts they burst out of the stable doors knocking over some of the patrol.

"Heyaaah! Another day Bon Varlet, Your time is coming!" declares Athos as the Musketeers make their escape at a full gallop.

"Damn you Musketeers. This is not over Athos!" shouts back Bon Varlet over the noise and confusion as the town's people who have been hiding in their homes finally come out. They have little choice as the explosion has started a small fire. It will soon be out but it contributes to the commotion and helps cause the Black Patrol's horses to flee.

"Come on let's get out of here," commands Bon Varlet to his men.

The last thing they need is for the locals to figure out that they are the Cardinal's Guard. Unable to gather their dead they can at least avoid the living being questioned. The Cardinal's power is considerable in France and Bon Varlet knows he will be able to cover their involvement in this affair. He also knows that the Cardinal will not be at all happy with the failure of the Black Patrol and the other forces who failed to capture Latour because of the interference of four Musketeers. Laval, many of his men and even members of the Black Patrol have perished or been wounded while the Three Musketeers and D'artagnan have all escaped.

While Bon Varlet and his men run to the hills around Auray, D'artagnan helps Latour up to the deck of the "Acadia." Without delay the vessel begins to move away from Auray as soon as the three are aboard. The ship's direction is of little interest to D'artagnan however. Once aboard he runs to the end of the ship for the best view of the shore. The last site he sees of the small coastal port is his friends riding away from danger. A broad smile crosses his face.

"Ride my friends! Ride, ha, ha, ha," The relieved adventurer bellows although it is unlikely they can hear him.

He knows exactly what they will do. They will ride quickly to their friend halfway to Paris to attend to Porthos and retrieve their own horses. They had switched mounts the day before on their way to Auray to speed their journey. From there, once Porthos is well enough, they will return to Paris to report to Tre'ville that Lady Latour is safe. They will not be able to report Bon Varlet's evil to the King as that would reveal their own involvement in this affair. Bon Varlet will not be eager to bring to light what has happened in Auray this night either and it will fade from history for most.

"Your friends are they safe?" asks Francoise with concern in her voice.

"They are," answers D'artagnan, unable to hide the relief in his voice.

"What now?" continues Latour.

"Well it looks like I am going to be taking a journey to the New World," answers the young Musketeer as his eye brows rise. "It appears I am all the help you were able to gather."

"You have already done so much. I'm sorry we cannot risk returning to France right now but as soon as we can we will take you home," she apologizes.

"Home, my Lady, is where the adventure is," he declares.

Three days have passed since the bloody battle in Auray. Three days of worry for Bon Varlet. His Black Patrol is in shambles and his quarry has escaped. As he sits in a hallway in the Cardinal's residence, his mind races with excuses. Bon Varlet is no coward but even he fears Richelieu.

"The Cardinal will see you now," comes a voice from a recently opened door.

Varlet did not even hear the Cardinal's aid coming. He does not answer but enters the large office sheepishly.

"Your grace," Bo Varlet says bowing.

"Stand up my good Count. I trust you have good news for me," he answers.

After a quick look at the Count's face the Cardinal continues. "No you do not do you? I sense your mission did not go well."

The Cardinal turns to his aid. "Leave us," he commands as he turns from them both and walks to his desk to have a seat. It is a large desk befitting the man who practically runs France.

"My mission was... uh a partial success. We were able to prevent the Lady Latour from gathering any support from her allies," Bon Varlet boasts.

"And where is the lady now?" probes Richelieu already knowing that he will not like the answer.

Bon Varlet pauses as Richelieu continues, lowering his face and looking up with his dark eyes. "Well, speak up man!"

"She has escaped" he answers softly. "She had help sir, Musketeers, At least ten." He says louder.

His lie does little to change the angry look on Richelieu's face.

"Are you not the man they call the Musketeer Killer?" asked the Cardinal. "I gave you enough men to handle twenty Musketeers and you still let her escape," accuses the Cardinal as Bon Varlet squirms.

"They were led by D'artagnan your grace," he mentions in hopes of saving face.

The Cardinals face tightens "D'artagnan! He and his friends have become a constant thorn in my side. I would have them arrested for their interference in this but that would expose my own part in this affair,"

"Surely d'Aulnay can handle Latour's forces now that they have failed to attain help," says Bon Varlet.

"You had better hope so my good Count. I am not pleased with this failure. Your family's fortunes have been fading for years. I could easily reverse their path but I am beginning to wonder why I should," reminds Richelieu.

"Sir I have served you faithfully. Just say the word and I will deal with D'artagnan, Athos and the others," offers Bon Varlet.

"Not yet. You need to lay low for now. Let the events in Auray fade into memory. I have much to do to erase the involvement of my Guard from this episode. You will get another chance Bon Varlet but for now return to your chalet and await my instructions," The Cardinal instructs

"Yes my grace. I await your summons," states the relieved Count.

"Until then you may want to practice your swordsmanship. D'artagnan has bested my finest guardsmen and I tire of losing to that child from Gascony." grunts Richelieu.

Bon Varlet nods, bows and exits the Cardinal's office quickly feeling lucky to have escaped the full force of Richelieu's anger.

The journey to the New World takes over thirty days. All in all not too bad and for D'artagnan it is a chance to get to know Francoise Marie Jacqelin Latour, Pierre Arsenault and the Acadia's captain, Armand Leblanc. He could not help but have his respect for the beautiful young Lady Latour increase with each day. Energetic, confident and most of all kind, she holds both the respect and affection of her men. All of whom keep a polite distance as Francoise is a happily married woman. Even D'artagnan who has on at least one occasion shown a willingness to ignore wedding vows makes no inappropriate moves. Still he cannot help but grow fond of the young woman who is his host on this crossing.

When the seas are not too rough they sit on the deck sipping wine and talking. Mostly they talk about her husband's dreams for Acadia. She is clearly invested in this dream and speaks of Charles with great affection. Her separation from him while necessary is obviously difficult for her. The failure to obtain help from her allies in France eats at her more with each passing day. Her love for her husband is almost equaled by her disdain for his rival "Charles De Menou d'Aulnay." There is no comparing the two men.

d'Aulnay's success has little to do with a dream or determination. He has benefited greatly from his association to Cardinal Richelieu. As the Cardinal grows more and more powerful d'Aulnay rises as well. It is a pattern D'artagnan has seen before. The two men do not look at all alike from what the crew tells the young Musketeer. Latour is a tall fit man who commands respect with his leadership ability. D'Aulnay is not the same hands on type. Overweight and often over dressed for the wild, he lacks anything that would attract the attention of young women. He is married but rumor has it that this is a political union. D'artagnan does not doubt this as everything surrounding d'Aulnay reeks of politics and intrigue. The loss of life that was the result of skirmishes west of Fort Latour and near Port Royal between their forces troubles the Latours but they doubt d'Aulnay will hesitate from launching another attack regardless of the human cost.

D'artagnan also finds time to get to know young Pierre Arsenault, the brave and loyal fourteen year old cabin boy who refused to leave the Lady Latour in Auray when the Cardinal's men were everywhere. It amazes him that Pierre seems as dedicated to honing his skills with a knife as D'aartagnan is with a pistol or Rapier. Only during a particularly nasty two day storm does the youth fail to keep his daily practice regime. Pierre clearly views the Captain as the father he never knew and Francoise like an older sister. The Captain took in the young starving orphan when he was docked in Marseille. In those days the gruff Captain was trading in the Mediterranean. Pierre was surviving by begging and stealing from the cities' rich. An attempt to relieve a wealthy Baron of his purse nearly cost Pierre his life. He barely escaped by stowing away on Captain Leblanc's previous ship. Leblanc took pity on the wretch and set about reforming him. It was not a difficult task. Poor Pierre had been shown little kindness in his life and the then nine year old reacted favourably to the Sea Captain's positive encouragement. Both the Captain and Pierre have proven staunch allies to the Latours.

...they sit on the deck sipping wine...

D'artagnan is closer to Pierre's age than the other men and the youth often follows him around when he is not practising or performing his ships duties. The dashing Lieutenant happily obliges Pierre's request for stories about his Musketeer adventures and his child hood in Gascony. Perhaps most impressive is how well read and capable the young cabin boy is academically. This is thanks to both to the Captain and the Latours. For two hours of each day they insist he continue his studies.

The longer D'artagnan is aboard the Acadia the less he misses home. The journey is a break from the danger of his everyday life. As much as he loves his life, this pleasant break would become a treasured memory in the years to come. Soon they would pass by Newfoundland, stopping long enough to fish for the seemingly endless cod fish that dominate the waters around the south of this large rocky island. From there it is on to Nova Scotia. This is d'Aulnay's domain and they take a wide arch around the tip of the mainland and stay on the north side of the Bay of Fundy.

Sailing on a clear morning they finally reach their destination. Near the mouth of the Saint John River where it meets the Bay is the log structure named Fort Latour. Well-constructed, if not large, it brings a huge smile from the petit and beautiful Lady Latour. It is a smile that grows even larger when she sees her husband come to greet her. Tall with long black hair, Latour presents an imposing image. His mustache is not unlike the many others worn by French nobles of this time.

Once the ship is anchored, the crew cannot lower a small boat fast enough for her. Their reunion is a warm and happy occasion but Charles Latour's expression changes a bit when he realizes that D'artagnan is the only new face among the crew. He receives a brief explanation from his bride before turning to the young Musketeer. As the crew unloads what supplies they had gathered at a stop just south of Aulay, Charles invites D'artagnan and Francoise into his cabin within the fort.

"I understand I owe you a great debt Lieutenant," he says.

"Not at all, any opportunity to stick it to Richelieu and his allies is a gift in my mind" replies D'artagnan.

"Indeed" responds a smiling Latour. None the less I am sorry my wife and crew could not safely drop you off before heading home."

"I have come to believe that I am just where I was intended to be. There is much good I can do here," proclaims D'artagnan.

Lowering his head and revealing a hint of shame, Charles Latour confides his sins to the brave D'artagnan. "I am afraid I must confess that I am not completely innocent in this conflict. The competition for Acadia has pushed both sides to violence. I was given a commission to rule Acadia by King Louis XIII himself but a year later Cardinal Richelieu granted the same lands to his cousin Isacc De Razilly. We came to a gentleman's agreement to keep the peace; after all there was wealth for all in the fur trade with the Indians. Once d'Aulnay took Razilly's place the peace ended. d'Aulnay is a ruthless and ambitious man who will stop at nothing to control this entire region. I am afraid I have displayed a knack for ruthlessness as well."

"No Charles! You are a good man and this land was granted to you by the King himself. None of this would have happened if not for the Cardinal's constant undercutting of the King," expresses Charles' loyal wife.

"The lady is right Charles. May I call you Charles?" asks D'artagnan.

Latour nods yes and D'artagnan continues. "You may be a little out of touch with all the intrigue back in France but I assure you Richelieu is behind almost all of it. His lust for power is a constant threat to the King and his allies. Unfortunately he has the King fooled and Louis considers the Cardinal one of his closest allies. If you are up against the Cardinal then you are on the side of right and a friend of the Musketeers," proclaims D'artagnan.

"I appreciate all you have said and all you have done. Know that we consider you a friend as well. This Acadian civil war has gone on for close to five years. I believe d'Aulnay is eager to end it. A recent raid on him by my forces was costly to him. It may have been retaliation for his own raid on one of my outpost's, but he will not care. He views his claim as more valid than mine and Richelieu the true power in France. He will attack again and without the reinforcements from my allies in France I have only one choice," says Charles Latour.

"I know enough about you to know that surrender is not that option," says D'artagnan.

"Indeed, I will never surrender to that dog. After a few days of rest for the crew I will take the Acadia to Boston to hire Mercenaries. I will have no problem recruiting the right kind of men there," explains Latour.

"Boston it is then," chimes in D'artagnan.

"I must ask you to stay here. I will face no danger in Boston but Fort Latour is under almost constant threat. I would feel better knowing a man with your experience in battle was here."

"Of course, whatever you think is best," offers our hero.

With that the conversation turns to tales of the adventures shared in Aulay. Joined by Pierre and the Captain for supper, it is a celebration of safe return.

Over the next few days D'artagnan's respect and affection for the Latours only grows as he watches how much they enjoy each other's company. Theirs may have been an arranged marriage but it has grown into something much more. Strengthened by Francoise's constant support for Charles' dreams of a united Acadian colony and helped along greatly by a mutual attraction for each other. The brave and hardy men who populate this new world are an inspiration to D'artagnan. He has heard about this new world but now he has the chance to see it with his own eyes. The Indians who canoe down the river to trade are strange to the young Musketeer but they too earn his respect. He cannot help but ask Pierre why Latour has not recruited the Mi'kmaq to fight on his side. The simple answer is that the natives have been trading with both sides and consider the Frenchman's war none of their business.

Less than a week has passed since they arrived and it is Sunday. The center of the log fort is transformed into an outdoor church as the inhabitants of this fortress celebrate mass. While not deeply religious D'artagnan attends, but he sits quietly at the back. This is more Aramis's type of gathering he thinks. Charles delivers the sermon and much of it is about the journey to find help in a roundabout way. Charles and Francoise retire shortly after the service and no one attempts to bother them with anything. They must once again be separated and the men understand that they need time to themselves.

On Monday Charles Latour and Captain Leblanc set sail for Boston leaving behind a small force and a very melancholy Lady Latour. She is not the only one trying to hide their sadness. Pierre's efforts to hide his displeasure with being left behind on this trip fail. Everyone can see the disappointment in his face.

"Come Pierre you have your studies to attend to," directs the Lady.

"Yes mademoiselle," answers the teen sheepishly.

Boston seems like an exciting place from what he has heard. Much more interesting than his studies he thinks. His protests all fall on deaf ears as Captain Leblanc strongly supported Francoise's wish to keep young Pierre at Fort Latour.

The days pass quietly at first. D'artagnan was given the job of making a daily trek to the top of a local rocky hill to watch for sails on the horizon, Latours or d'Aulnay's. Mostly at this time it was d'Aulnay's ships that concerned them since Latour would not be back this soon. The hill was about a mile and a half away and they consider building a cabin there and taking turns staying in it to keep an eye on the entrance to the harbour.

It is decided that they are too short staffed for that now. So every day D'artagnan makes the trek, usually alone. Today however will be different.

"Please My Lady I have been studying hard. Just this one day may I go with D'artagnan?" pleads Pierre.

"Pierre please you know how important your studies are," replies Francoise.

Feeling sorry for the young lad D'artagnan intercedes, "My lady if you would like I could go over some of his work with him once we reach the top of the hill."

Latour first scoffs and then smiles as she sees the hopeful look on Pierre. "Alright, I guess the boy could use a break. Leave you books behind and go with D'artagnan," says Francoise. "But tomorrow it is back to your studies," she warns.

"Thank you," beams an elated Pierre as he runs to grab his musket.

"You really must stop encouraging the boy," smiles Francoise.

"He will be a man soon my Lady and he needs a little action. Besides in this land there are many things he must be taught that he cannot learn from a book," reminds the buckskin clad adventurer.

It seems strange to D'artagnan to be wearing such attire but it is both common and practical here. Beside it is not like he had time to pack before sailing. The journey to the lookout point starts with a short canoe ride to the west side of the harbour. After being dropped off by one of Latour's men they begin the mostly uphill hike through thick woods. Pierre talks the entire walk which comes as no surprise to D'artagnan. Once they arrive at their destination they take turns scanning the horizon with an old spy glass.

"This was the Captain's but it's in rough shape now and he has a new one so he gave it to me," Pierre explains.

"It still works, which makes it a nice gift," notes D'artagnan."

"Yeah," replies a smiling Pierre.

The two continue to take turns watching for a possible raiding or invasion party. At one point D'artagnan thinks he has heard something in the thick brush nearby and grabs his Musket but after investigating decides it is in his head and goes back to the task at hand.

"What was it?" inquires Pierre who is also grasping his weapon.

"Nothing, I just thought I heard something. It was probably just a rabbit." Answers D'artagnan.

"Want me to see if I can get it. Rabbit makes for a good lunch" He asks as he motions to the small fire they had started just ten minutes before.

"No, we have a lunch packed. Let's keep to our task," replies the young Musketeer.

Only a little disappointed by his friends decision Pierre turns back to look at the bay.

"Hey, I think I see something!" he says.

"What let me see!" barks D'artagnan as he grabs the spy glass from the young teen. Lifting it to his eye he cannot see anything at first.

"Where Pierre, I don't see anything?" he asks with a concern in his voice. An attack could be a disaster with the undermanned fort.

"To the left, over there," directs Pierre as points to where he thought he saw a sail.

"No! I see it, a sail or maybe two," he exclaims. Handing the glass back to Pierre he starts to grab his gun and sack. "Keep an eye on it for a minute. We have to warn the......Aaaagh!" screams a startled D'artagnan.

Surprised by the sudden and blood curdling scream by his friend Pierre turns to see a nightmare. A large male black bear had managed to sneak up on them while they were concerned with the sails in the distance.

"No D'artagnan!" yells a suddenly frozen Pierre as he watches his friend desperately try to fend off the hungry carnivore with the butt of his Musket.

"Your gun... argh! Shoot it!" commands the wounded and bloody man.

Jolted from his shock by the intensity of D'artagnan's shout, Pierre lunges for his nearby musket. Already loaded from earlier when D'artagnan had heard something in the woods he gets off a quick shot from close range striking the bear in his shoulder. It lets out a loud and mournful sound as it rails backwards. Much to Pierre's horror the fierce killer does not go down and turns to the frightened youth and stands on his hind legs. In this upright position he is easily over six foot. Mustering all the courage he can manage Pierre quickly pulls two of his knives from the special holster vest around his shoulder and throws them into the bear's stomach. The bear moans again and drops back down to four legs but again refuses to die. After a loud roar he moves quickly to strike Pierre. Words cannot describe the terror one feels when faced with one of these merciless beast. Pierre is again frozen and believes he is about to die when he hears a shot ring out. Finally the creature falls landing only one foot from the traumatized boy. The first thing Pierre sees is blood pouring from the bear's head. The young man looks past the black bear to see D'artagnan on his knees with his smoking Musket in hand. Pierre instantly realizes that it was his friend who saved him.

"Pierre," D'artagnan quietly mutters, then falls forward unconscious.

"D'artagnan!" calls Pierre but his saviour cannot hear him.

D'artagnan is bleeding badly from his chest and it is clear to Pierre that the bear must have got in a quick swipe when he snuck up on them. It is a miracle that he had the strength to hold off the beast. Acting as quickly as he can to stop the bleeding Pierre forgets all about the approaching vessels. He had seen Captain Leblanc and the ships cooks treat a badly wounded sailor once and had a little knowledge of what to do. Taking a stick from the fire he burns the worst of the wounds to stop the flow of blood.

"Arrrgh!" shrieks D'artagnan, as he momentarily is jolted back to consciousness.

He is not long passing out again and Pierre continues to work on him by applying cloth and pressure to the wounds. Somehow it is enough and in a reasonable amount of time he is able to stop the flow of life giving blood. Relieved and somewhat proud of his work Pierre allows himself a small smile. It is short lived. From down the great hill to the east he hears the sudden and unmistakable sound of cannon fire.

"The fort, no! I forgot about the sails." He begins to head towards the sound of fighting but is stopped by the painful moans from D'artagnan.

Torn he looks back to his friend, then towards the area of the fort. Again D'artagnan reels in pain and Pierre rushes to his side to calm him. It is then he knows what he must do. The men in the fort may be able to fend of d'Aulnay's men but D'artagnan will not survive without him. Pierre must remain with his new friend.

By nightfall the sound of battle subsides. Pierre can see much of it from his perch at the top of the hill. Nearby D'artagnan lays unconscious and still. He is covered by both blankets as Pierre knows the importance of keeping him warm. While the night is a bit colder it is not winter and there is no danger of anyone freezing. In order to avoid discomfort Pierre takes his small hatchet and cuts off branches from a Douglas fir tree to cover himself with. The resourceful young man knows enough to douse his fire so that d'Aulnay's men could not see it. He is glad that D'artagnan always insists on bringing at least some supplies with him when he is on watch duty. A hatchet, two blankets and a small amount of food is not much but it has all come in handy.

The next day D'artagnan wakes long enough to eat but is still dazed and weak. When he fades back into much needed sleep Pierre decides he must find out what is happening at the fort. Covering his friend with both the blankets and some branches to hide him from predators he begins the trek downhill towards the sound of musket fire. The battle has begun anew and Pierre's concern for the Lady and her men is overwhelming. If only D'artagnan had not been hurt, he would know what to do, the lad thinks.

The journey down to the west side of the harbour is quicker but seems to take forever. Careful to remain unseen Pierre crawls carefully to a spot near where they had been dropped off by canoe. From this close point he can clearly see just how desperate his friends' plight is. D'Aulnay is personally leading the assault. The villainous nobleman does not present the same kind of imposing figure as Charles Latour. He is overweight and fairly short. Over dressed for a battle he keeps his distance from the fighting, commanding his troops from a safe distance. He is however close enough that Pierre might be able to hit him with a well-aimed musket shot. The thought does not stay in his mind long. Pierre knows he is not yet skilled enough to make such a shot and if he was discovered D'artagnan is as good as dead. If only d'Aulnay was within range for Pierre's knives. He never misses with his blades. More concerning than d'Aulnay's personal involvement in this attack is the number of men he commands. The small defense force is badly outnumbered. This is clearly an attempt to end the Acadian Civil War in one fell swoop. Why has God abandoned us thinks Pierre. The bear's attack meant they were unable to warn the Fort and Charles' journey has left the fort under defended. It is as if the fates have conspired to aid d'Aulnay's nefarious plans.

Catching himself from falling into despair and losing faith in God, Pierre remembers all that Francoise has taught him. She would not be happy with him questioning his Lord. It is then that he sees her. There she stands on the ramparts as clear as day, The Lady Latour rallying her men. Firing and reloading with as much skill as any man could. She refuses to hide and is a target for d'Aulnay's vultures but somehow they cannot seem to hit her. She on the other hand has little trouble hitting her targets. Several other muskets can be seen from the small holes in the fort's wall that have been cut to allow just such a defense. The sight of the Lady in all her courage and glory fills Pierre with hope. When this recent round of attacks ends he crawls back away from the shore and then makes his way back to the hill. It is not the only hill in the area and his trek is not easy.

Once back to his camp he sees D'artagnan trying to get to his feet.

"D'artagnan wait, "he yells.

"The fort, I must get to the fort," he manages.

He can barely stand but summons what little strength he has in a valiant effort to aid his friends. It is a futile effort and he falls. Pierre reaches him just in time to catch him before he hits the ground.

"D'artagnan, ugh," Pierre mutters as he struggles to hold up the notice-ably larger man. Laying him down as gently as he can, Pierre then rushes to bring him a drink of water.

"Here drink this," he says as the distraught Musketeer grasps for a drink.

"The Fort, Lady Latour. What is happening?" He says pleading for answers.

Pierre's heart sinks as he knows he must tell his friend the truth.

"It is bad my friend. D'Aulnay is leading a large force. Somehow they have been repelled several times but I fear for the Lady and our men," he tells D'artagnan as he fights back tears.

The past two days have been the worst of his often troubled life and all Pierre wants to do is let go and cry. He will not however, not in front of the King's Musketeer. Not in front of this man who he admires so much.

"I must get to the fort. Get me to my feet" orders D'artagnan, but Pierre does not comply.

"No, you are in no shape for battle. You cannot even make it down the hill in your condition," protests Pierre in as stern a voice as he can manage. "You must rest. Tomorrow I will go and try to get close enough to pick off d'Aulnay. Without him the others will not continue the attack," Pierre explains.

D'artagnan knows that the boy is right about his condition and he also know that such an attempt will bring about the young man's death."

"No Pierre, you must stay with me until I am well enough. Then we will go together. I just need a little more rest," D'artagnan says knowing this will stop the lad from his reckless plan.

Shortly after D'artagnan is laid back on his blankets and falls into unconsciousness again. Knowing his friend will need food and with little supplies left Pierre sets out to gather some. Wild berries and apples from nearby trees will have to do as hunting is out of the question. A gunshot would only draw attention to them and they could not risk a cooking fire anyway. Once the food is gathered, Pierre sets about building a lean too. A small shelter he learned to build from "Lucien" one of Latour's best men. Pierre briefly remembers that Lucien is one of the men trapped in the Fort. Pushing that thought from his mind he finishes his work. As the darkness comes it is welcome for more than one reason. Pierre is exhausted and needs sleep but mostly the sounds of fighting ceases when the sun goes down. Pierre is not sure how the Lady and her men are holding out or how long they can fend off d'Aulnay and his much larger force. The thoughts of what may happen if he breaks through makes sleeping difficult but Pierre

"....I fear for the Lady and our men..."

is beyond tired and does manage to sleep.

In the morning Pierre is surprised to see that D'artagnan is awake before him and eating some of the berries that Pierre had gathered.

"You're awake," states D'artagnan.

"Barely," answers the lad before he sits up quickly at the sound of renewed fighting at the fort. "The fort! What is happening?" He asks.

"I'm not sure, the fighting just began," Replies D'artagnan. "

"I need to find out," says the concerned young man.

"I know but eat first. You'll need your strength," sighs D'artagnan.

The distraught Musketeer is slightly better than the day before but he knows he is still in no shape for combat. He is not sure he could make the hike to the shore even with help. He cannot save the fort's defenders but he can save the boy.

"Pierre I know you are going to return to the river's mouth to see what is happening but you cannot help them. Promise me you will not take part in the fighting."

"But…," protest Pierre before he gets cut off.

"Listen to me Pierre, there is nothing you can do. If you get captured you can be used to force Lady Latour to surrender. Even worse if you are killed it could break her will. Their best hope is for Charles to return sooner than expected or for d'Aulnay to be shot and killed," explains the wounded man.

"d'Aulnay is a coward! He hides behind his men too far from the fighting to be hit," growls Pierre.

"Pierre you must not do anything rash. Getting yourself killed will solve nothing. Promise me you will only scout the situation," gasps the weakening adult.

"I…I promise", answers the teen reluctantly.

After a quick and mostly silent breakfast, Pierre begins the trip down the hills to where the river meets the bay. It is high tide now. The Bay of Fundy has the highest tides in the world. It is so powerful that at high tide it actually forces the great river back. The currents are too strong for swimming in the Saint John River and even if Pierre tried to join his friends he would not be able to make the crossing. As he nears the battle zone he is alarmed by how fierce the fighting sounds. His concerns are confirmed as he crawls to where he can see the fort. d'Aulnay is launching an all-out assault. Their ship's cannon has helped them breach the fort's walls. Valiantly Latour's small band once again repels the invaders but it is clear that they cannot hold out any longer.

Desperate and with little hope left Lady Latour calls out to her attackers.

Pierre can hear just enough of hers and d'Aulnay's shouts to know what is going on. She is offering surrender with only one condition. She will give d'Aulnay the fort if he will spare her men. It seems a reasonable request and d'Aulnay has lost enough men these last three days. To Pierre's relief d'Aulnay accepts her terms. Latour's men throw out their muskets as instructed. Finally d'Aulnay comes out from his safe position to march proudly into Fort Latour. What he sees enrages him. Having been pushed back many times he expected a large defense force. What he finds is eleven men and Lady Latour.

"Where are the others?" He screams so loud that even Pierre can hear him from across the rivers.

Pierre cannot hear Lady Latour's answer but she is clearly telling him that this is all of her men. d'Aulnay goes berserk. Throwing his hat and smashing one of the surrendered muskets. Latour tries to calm him but it is a useless effort. What happens next is one of the darkest events in the history of the New World. d'Aulnay orders all of the men in the fort hanged. Lady Latour desperately pleads for their lives but d'Aulnay is out of control. One by one they are strung from the fort's ramparts as Francoise is forced to watch. This is D'Aulnay's payment for the embarrassment of being kept out of the fort so long.

Pierre cannot bear to see it all. He crawls back through the brush after the first hanging. His last memory is the scream of Lady Latour as Lucien is hanged. He cannot hold back the tears any longer. They flow from his face like a waterfall. Even once he makes it to the camp and is facing the man who has become his hero he cannot control his emotions. D'artagnan's attempts to calm the boy are futile. The Lady and her men were his family and now many of them are gone. D'artagnan cannot fight back tears as well; although he has a lump is in his throat.

It takes several attempts before Pierre can get the full story out. Richelieu has chosen his Governor well D'artagnan thinks. He is a man with as black a heart as the Cardinal himself. D'artagnan reassures Pierre that there is nothing he could have done. In five days when he is well enough D'artagnan and Pierre go to the fort to attempt a rescue of Francoise but it is too late. They capture one of d'Aulnay's men and learn that Lady Latour died the day before in captivity. Legend would tell that she died of a broken heart and in truth it may be true.

After sending Pierre back to their camp on the hill so he does not see, D'artagnan dispatches of the man. He does not even try to convince himself that he kills him to protect the secret of their location. D'artagnan feels an anger he has never experienced and someone was going to pay for d'Aulnay's evil deeds.

In another day d'Aulnay returns with his force to Port Royal across the large bay and D'artagnan and Pierre come down from the forest. Short days later Charles Latour returns aboard the "Acadia." D'artagnan must be the one to tell him of his wife's fate. Latour is inconsolable. The great leader is instantly broken by a tragedy that would take down any man with a heart. D'artagnan briefly wonders if that heart makes him stronger or weaker than d'Aulnay in a time of war. He knows the answer of course. A heart that knows love is always stronger but in times like these it breaks like glass thrown against a wall. In his grief Charles vows revenge but he had not been able to hire enough mercenaries and has lost many of his best men in the battle of Fort Latour. D'Aulnay has won the war. In Pierre's opinion winning the fight for Acadia will cost d'Aulnay his soul. Charles sails the Acadia to Quebec City and seeks refugee in the Chateau Saint Louis from "Charles Jacques Huault De Montmagny" the Governor of New France. D'Aulnay becomes the lone Governor of Acadia.

Even in his grief Latour has compassion for others especially young Pierre. Once he has booked passage back to Europe for D'artagnan he asks the Musketeer to bring the young man with him to Paris to continue his studies. Pierre refuses at first but Charles and Captain Leblanc convince him that it is what Francoise would want. The young teen is damaged and hardened by the events of the past month but he is still a very bright and resourceful young man. With the backing of Latour, Montmagny, Tre'ville and others he will go on to a bright future. In the time he stays in Quebec, Pierre is helped greatly with his grief by the priests who are part of this young colony. D'artagnan's faith in God is somewhat less than the youth's and the death of Lady Latour has pushed him farther from a relationship with God than ever before. Such things are best left to Aramis he thinks to himself. It is a thought that goes through his mind often.

The journey home is slightly shorter than the voyage to the New World was but it seems much longer. D'artagnan takes up the job of making sure Pierre continues with his studies. Once back in France, D'artagnan is comforted by his friends who are aware of much of what has transpired through letters sent on a ship that left just days before D'artagnan's. The tortured Musketeer fills in the rest of the sad tale. As all good friends do, they allow him his tears.

D'artagnan delivers Pierre to the private school Latour had requested. He keeps Charles Latour's request that he visit the boy as often as he can.

He does so not to keep a promise however but because he cares about the orphan who showed so much courage and love for his friends.

Charles Latour's destiny is not complete yet nor is the fate of Acadia but that is another story. This story is not quite over yet either. D'Aulnay may be too far away and too powerful to touch right now but there is another villain who is not. D'artagnan is determined to both make someone pay and to weaken the villainous Cardinal Richelieu. He does not have to wait long.

As D'artagnan and the three Musketeers practice in the court yard of the Musketeer headquarters they are summoned to Captain Tre'ville's office.

"I have a job for you but this time I am going with you," begins Tre'ville. "Bon Varlet has struck again. Yesterday he killed yet another Musketeer, The sixth that we know of. This time we have proof that he was involved."

"I knew the snake would trip up eventually," comments Athos. "But who is it that he has murdered this time?" he asks.

"Young Lafeyette I'm afraid. The young man never had a chance. Two of Bon Varlet's Black Patrol were with the dark Count," reports Tre'ville.

"The murderer, I can take no more. He will pay," promises Porthos.

"Yes Porthos, he will pay but we must arrest him quickly before Richelieu can get to our witnesses. I have sent a troop to protect them but both Richelieu and Bon Varlet have endless resources. The faster we have the Count in our custody the better," Tre'ville cautions.

"He will not be taken alive. It is not his way," warns Aramis

"I know Aramis that is why you will be with me when we go to his family's home. He has killed too many Musketeers. If it comes to a fight I want him to face our best," Says Tre'ville.

"I will handle him," states Athos.

"No, he is mine. If it was not for Richelieu and Bon Varlet's interference Lady Latour would have been able to gather enough men to defend against d'Aulnay and she might still be alive," D'artagnan reminds them.

"But…" Athos begins to protest.

"Please my friend I need to do this. I was not able to help save the defenders of Fort Latour but I can at least avenge one of their enemies. Let me have Bon Varlet." pleads D'artagnan.

"All right D'artagnan. If anyone other than me can defeat the serpent it is you. If he resists he is yours," promises Athos.

"It is decided then. We ride as soon as our horses are saddled. We'll take twenty men with us and gather up other Musketeers as we go," Tre'ville orders.

Through the Paris streets ride the valiant Musketeers. Some cheer as they gallop by, others just stop and smile. One person is not impressed or pleased at the sight. From a window in his office Cardinal Richelieu watches the posse speed by.

"Sir, should I send word to Bon Varlet that the Musketeers may be gathering to arrest him?" asks the Cardinal's aid.

"He knows Frances, he knows. The Musketeers would be upon him before we could get a rider there anyway. He is a faithful agent Frances but he is often reckless and he has been headed towards a show down with the Musketeers for some time," deduces the red garbed cleric.

"Then I suppose all we can do is pray. I am sure if Bon Varlet can fend off this attack we will have time to find a way out of his legal problems," Frances says

"That is a considerable If. I could see who was riding with Tre'ville. I am afraid it could go either way. We may lose a key ally this day," admits the Cardinal.

Once out of the city Tre'ville's posse adds to its numbers. Word had been sent out for other Musketeers on missions to meet up with them on the road. They fall in line at full gallop as the formidable force grows to thirty. Once at Bon Varlet's Chalet they stop just out of musket range. One last Musketeer on horseback joins the troop. It is dark now so his information is of great value.

"I arrived ahead of you Captain and have been able to scout the Count's defenses." reports Raymond Audette.

"Report Musketeer," orders Tre'ville.

"He has his reinforced Black Patrol plus thirty more, mostly mercenaries. We are a bit outnumbered and they have cover behind the four foot fence around his Chalet," warns Audette.

"So the Cardinal could or would not send more of his guardsmen. Very well, no Mercenary or Cardinal's guard has ever been the equal of a Musketeer," boasts Tre'ville.

"We could surround the estate but they could hold on for a long time, Time that Richelieu could use to turn the King in his favour," adds D'artagnan.

"My thought exactly. We'll do what they don't expect, a full charge on horseback. We'll use grenades to break down the gate and cause confusion. Porthos and Aramis will lead with the grenades. The rest of you give them as much cover fire as possible," orders Tre'ville.

With that, the Musketeers line up and wait for the order.

"Charge!" yells the Captain and with that command the brave Musketeers all urge their tired mounts forward for a full speed attack.

Bon Varlet's men open fire felling three of Tre'ville's comrades but the others ride forward without hesitation. It is not every day that Tre'ville leads his men in the field and none of the Musketeers wants to be the one to break ranks. The first to reach the wall as planned are Aramis and Porthos who throw their grenades at the old gate breaking it open. By now some Musketeers including Athos and D'artagnan have beaten them to the attack by jumping the fence, plunging themselves into the defenders. Shots ring out from both sides as Bon Varlet's men from the far side of the house rush to the front to help their compatriots. They can do little to turn the tide of the Musketeers' bold attack. With their first shots spent the warriors turn to hand to hand and sword to sword combat. Everywhere on the great lawn in front of the Chalet dismounted Musketeers fan out and choose sparing partners. Porthos finds himself one against two but dispatches of the first so quickly that the other momentarily steps back in shock.

"Don't go away my good man you're next," Porthos taunts.

Reacting to the challenge the mercenary lunges at his prey but a smiling Porthos turns to his side causing the blade to miss. Porthos however does not miss and buries his rapier in the man's side.

"Somebody save me a Cardinal's guard, these Mercenaries die too easily," he requests.

One fighter who does not dismount is D'artagnan who forces his way past two Guardsmen who are blocking the front door. Both are knocked to their knees as D'artagnan's great stallion busts open the door and strides into a large open area with a staircase to the right side. In the center stands Bon Varlet with his pistol ready. He fires a shot but misses a ducking D'artagnan. As he dismounts D'artagnan draws his rapier challenging Bon Varlet.

"Defend yourself Bon Varlet," he demands.

"I have been waiting for the day I could test my skills against yours pup," claims Bon Varlet as he stabs at the young Musketeer.

"If so than why are you hiding in the chalet while your men do the fighting?" asks D'artagnan.

The question infuriates Bon Varlet and he thrusts carelessly at D'artagnan who manages to cut Varlet's arm. His shirt and arm are both the worse for wear.

"Ah! Tre'ville's dog! I did not expect such a quick attack or I would have met you at the gate," he barks as he holds his other hand over the cut.

Just then three of Varlet's Black Patrol bust in and draw D'artagnan's attention. D'artagnan fends them off as he backs up the long winding stairs. It is a wise move as the stairs are not wide enough for all three to attack at once. Just then Athos, Aramis and Porthos hurry in to aid their friend. As the Guardsmen turn to defend themselves D'artagnan jumps onto the chandelier and swings to block an escaping Bon Varlet, landing just in front of him.

"Going somewhere?" asks D'artagnan.

Bon Varlet is panicked now. Tre'ville and his men are winning the battle outside and D'artagnan blocks his escape.

"Out of my way you cursed Musketeer," he orders. But D'artagnan presses his attack.

"Richelieu's dog I'll make you pay," he replies as he cuts Varlet's other arm.

The cut is minor and Bon Varlet is still in the fight. Athos, Aramis and Porthos have defeated their foes and stand on the stair case watching.

"Finish him off D'artagnan," cheers Athos.

D'artagnan however is not done playing with is enemy. A brief pause in the fight gives him a chance to remind Bon Varlet of his sins. Bon Varlet is an expert swordsman as his reputation implies but no fighter has ever been more motivated than D'artagnan.

"This is for the Musketeers you have killed and for the Lady Latour." With that both men engage in a final assault on each other.

They end up just inches from each other's face. Each has a look of shock on their face. The Musketeers show concern at first but suddenly D'artagnan pulls back to reveal that his sword is lodged in Bon Varlet's mid-section and to show that the Cardinal's Dog has missed.

"No, it cannot be. I cannot die at the hands of a Musketeer," he says.

Then D'artagnan pulls his sword out of Bon Varlet's torso and watches him fall.

"Bravo D'artagnan," cheers Aramis as Tre'ville and two others rush in.

D'artagnan allows himself a brief smile and then drops his head a little. Revenge he realizes does not take away the pain of loss. Still he can take comfort in the fact that Bon Varlet and his Black Patrol will not have any more victims. It is not the complete victory he had hoped for when this adventure began but it is a victory indeed.

"Well done D'artagnan. I knew you could best him," Tre'ville congratulates as he pats the young hero on the shoulder.

D'artagnan smiles again knowing that every Musketeer is safer with Bon Varlet dead.

"Everyone in," orders Athos as he raises his sword.

The others raise theirs as well and point them all to the same spot over their heads causing them to cross. Tre'ville watches and smiles proudly.

"All for one," they say loudly and after a pause they finish their moto. "And one for all!"

Finis

About This Story

One of the interesting things about Alexander Dumas's Three Musketeers novels is the way in which he included real people. While most of the characters were fictional some such as the King and Queen were historical figures. It is said that even the main characters were based on actual Musketeers. Perhaps the most prominent figure in the first novel who was in fact a real person was Cardinal Richelieu. The ambitious and powerful Cardinal rose to the position of Chief or First Minister under King Louis XIII. Richelieu also plays a role in my story "The Lady of Acadia" which you have just read. In fact the powerful Cardinal's involvement in the history of my home town of Saint John New Brunswick Canada was what got the idea started in my head a few years back. You see the first real settlement in this area was called Fort Latour. The east coast of Canada at this time was called Acadia and was under French control. King Louis XIII awarded the region to Charles Latour and his young bride but then Richelieu gave the same land to Charles d'Aulnay sparking a conflict known as the Acadian civil war. Richelieu was also involved in preventing Lady Latour from being able to gather help for her husband when she briefly returned to France. I say briefly because it was not safe for her to stay there. It is around these events that I have spun my yarn of politics, love, loyalty, courage, adventure and, yes, tragedy. Make no mistake there is an element of tragedy as I have tried to remain true to many of the historical facts in this battle. I think you could argue that there is tragedy in any war and this little known conflict is no exception. Of course this is a Three Musketeers story so it is first and foremost an adventure. Weaved around the real people in this tale are fictional characters created by both Dumas and myself. I have also taken some artistic liberties with both the story and characters. This is, after all, mostly a work of fiction. Fans of Dumas' work need not worry as I have stayed true to his creations. I am, after all, a fan myself. So, in the tradition of Alexander Dumas I present this fictional tale of the Three Musketeers involvement in the very real battle of Fort Latour.

PAUL BEALE-is a versatile writer best known for his work in comic books and short stories. He was born in 1962 in Saint John New Brunswick Canada where he still lives to this day. Vivid daydreams of other worlds and people led him to draw and write comics as early as eleven years old. At first using other people's characters that were from the comic books he owned and then about his own creations. None of these early works were shared with anyone except family and friends but some of the concepts and characters found their way into his later published work.

In the mid 80's Paul had a chance meeting with another creator, Jim Hachey, who was about to publish a local comic. Jim recruited Paul to co - create, write, and draw a backup story series for the book. From there Paul continued to work in several small press publications in Eastern Canada including his own book "Third Wave." In 2014 a story of Paul's was published in Jim Hachey's "Manga Ganda" anthology by professional comic book company "Red Leaf Comics". After emailing Publisher John Helmer three more completed stories Paul was ask to edit and write "All Canadian Comics" for Red Leaf. He jumped at the chance. Since then he and his "All Comics Team" have added two more titles, "All Christian" and "All Action Hero" to the Red Leaf line. All edited, written and occasionally drawn by Paul with new issues coming out as this is being written. He has also written for "Advent Comics", "Pilot Studios", "Nerdanatix" and will soon be in "Charltoons" for "Charlton Neo" with several comic book legends. All have a strong online sales presence on sites like "Drive Thru Comics" as well as traditional paper copy sales. This has given Paul a chance to get his stories out there to an international audience. These stories fit into multiple genres like Superhero, World War II, Western, Pulp Hero, Sci Fi, Suspense, Christian, Teen Mystery, Jungle action Cartoon, and just about everything else.

Comics are not Paul's only published works. He has written short stories for the online Magazine "Sci Fi Max," whose online issues have had over 45,000 hits. Most recently Paul has written a 30 page "Three Musketeers" story which will soon be published by Airship 27 for an anthology pulp novel series. Airship is edited by former "Green Hornet" [Now comics] writer Ron Fortier.

Noblesse Oblige

By Alan J. Porter

France - 1635

"Dogs." La Porte muttered the word under his breath and spat as if it was a curse. He hated the creatures. His mother had owned a small dog that she doted on more than she did her son. Even now he could recall the way that dog smelt, its natural odors masked by constant bathing and perfumed oils applied with an almost indecently sensual relish. He remembered its shrill yapping bark demanding that its hunger be sated by the best cuts of meat in the house. And above all that the wretched animal was allowed free rein to expel its bodily fluids wherever it felt like, including on his bed coverings, a spot it had decided to make its own despite La Porte's obvious hostility towards it. No matter what he did that damned dog would not leave him alone.

He didn't come from a particularly wealthy family, they weren't poor, but they were a little short of comfortable, and a long way short of mixing with the level of society he now served. But his mother never was happy with her station in life and constantly strived, if not to improve herself, to at least to appear as if they had more than they really did. While he and his father made do with what they could afford, his mother insisted on keeping up appearances with extravagant dresses, outrageous hairpieces, costly perfumes, and that damn dog that went everywhere with her on the end of a silken leash with ribbons in its hair.

He had naturally grown up with an adversarial relationship with canines, especially small yappy ones that seemed to think that they deserved to be pampered and fed at the drop of a hat. But truth be told he wasn't that enamored of large dogs either, especially bad tempered hungry ones. Ones just like the pack that he could hear crashing through the undergrowth not too far from the tree in which he was currently perched.

From his vantage point he could see the umbrella of ferns on the woodland floor moving as the hounds moved to and fro in search of his scent. The half dozen bags of aniseed extract that he thrown in random directions as he'd ran off the cart track and deeper into the woods had helped confuse them and given him some respite. Looking down at the waving ferns he estimated that there must be at least half a dozen dogs, along with an equal number of handlers, plus one other man whose shouted orders marked him out as being in charge. La Porte wasn't sure who he was, but he knew why the man was hunting him. He was determined not to be caught under any circumstances. After all he had a reputation to maintain.

Pulling his eyes away from the forest floor and the approaching pack, he raised his gaze to survey the area around him.

His salvation lay about four hundred meters to the west. The break in the tree canopy suggested that a stream or river lay there, possibly a wide one. La Porte's hand slipped into the pouch hanging from his tunic belt. His fingers curled around the one remaining aniseed ball. He pulled himself up to a standing position on the large branch that had served as his observation post, braced his back against the mature tree's broad trunk, pulled back his right arm, and threw the aniseed as far in an eastward direction as he could. He didn't wait to follow its trajectory or track its landing point. As soon as the projectile left his finger tips he scrambled down the tree to the wood's floor and sprinted for the break in the trees hoping against hope that his intuition about what lay there served him well.

It did. For as he reached his target he found himself on the bank of a wide stream. Unfortunately any delight at this discovery was tempered by the fact that the ruse with his final aniseed ball had failed completely. His hasty descent from the tree and the noise of his following crashing rush through the undergrowth had attracted the attention of his human pursuers. The men called and cajoled their canine charges to ignore the false scent, and they were soon heading directly towards La Porte.

For the moment he remained unsighted to those who hunted him, but he knew that they would be on him in a few breaths. He really only had one option but there was a certain reluctance to undertake it.

He was proud of the clothes he now wore. After the years of make do, he had landed a position in which he, not his mother, mixed with the highest in the land. As such he had been provided with a wardrobe suitable to be seen amongst such company. It wasn't ostentatious or flamboyant, but it was good cloth, fit well, and he was proud of it. In fact he had become known for his almost fastidious attention to keeping his clothing clean and in perfect condition. Everyone knew that not a stain, mark, rent, or tear would be seen on La Porte. He glanced down at the state of his current attire and groaned in shame, for his clothing was marked with all those aforementioned blemishes. La Porte glanced back towards the approaching hounds. They wouldn't care for his sartorial reputation. They wanted one thing, and he had been entrusted with it. There was no choice.

La Porte pressed his hand against his doublet to make sure the stitched leather envelope was still pressed against his chest. Then he shrugged his shoulders, and dived head first into the stream.

He had miscalculated. The stream was fast flowing with a strong under-current, and it was shallow.

La Porte's head hit the boulder on the stream bed with a crack that was hard and painful enough for LaPorte to let out an involuntary gasp and fill his mouth with water just before he slipped into unconsciousness.

The undertow gripped his limp form, and La Porte was rapidly drawn away from those who hunted him.

"What do you mean he disappeared.?"

Captain Marc-Ange stood in silence. He knew there was little point in trying to defend himself to this man. He'd reported to him for over five years now, and these sort of encounters never got easier, even as they grew more frequent. It didn't matter what he said fault would be found, even if it had been a successful mission. When there had been a failure then this was a not a place you wanted to be.

Even though he'd been in this room numerous times over the last half-decade, too many to keep track of, he always looked around. Firstly as a soldier he had developed the habit of considering any space he found him-self in as a potential battle ground. Where was there room to fight, where didn't he want to get trapped, where did the light come from, what obsta-cles could be used for cover, where were the potential exit routes in case of escape? It was a habit that had served him well, and saved both him-self and the lives of several of his men over the years. As a result he'd become a popular troop leader, and had risen to his current rank. A rank he now wondered if he would still be wearing when he left this office today. The second reason he took a mental inventory of this space was that the annoyed man who sat behind the impressively large mahogany desk liked to play mind games by moving things around to destroy any sense of famil-iarity that anyone else may build up for what was his space, and his space alone. It was whispered that even the king would express delight when on visiting this office he noted that a particular statue or side table had been repositioned.

While Louis the monarch of France delighted at such seemingly frivolous games, it was the man who sat across the desk and played those games with a deadly purpose who truly ruled, Cardinal Richelieu, the first minister of France.

"You had a pack of my finest hunting dogs, and yet a simple courier eluded you."

The captain hung his head and stared at the floor awaiting the storm of displeasure to continue. He was not to be disappointed. The cardinal pushed back his chair, rose to his feet and brought the flat of his hand down on the leather that had been immaculately inlaid into the desktop surface. The resulting sound was a crack not unlike the sound of a whip. It made Marc-Ange flinch with its association. He was sure it had been designed, and the maneuver practiced, in a way just to produce such a result. He raised his head, and looked at the cardinal, although with his gaze averted from the minister's face. "We believe he fell into a stream and drowned. We found blood on a rock, but we couldn't find the body. It must have been carried away downstream."

"Then the letter he was carrying is lost." The voice was soft and low. A tone that carried way more menace than the screaming and shouting.

"I assume so my lord."

"Assume! Must have! Believe!" The voice remained low, almost a whisper. "These are not words I will not accept from my captains. Find that letter Marc-Ange or you will be sweeping the stables by the next sabbath."

Marc-Ange stood to attention where he was as the cardinal turned and walked away from him without another word. As the minister strode from the office the soldier watched his back. The man strode with purpose, his black ecclesiastical robes, made of the highest quality cloth, flowing around him. He wore no adornments or obvious signs of authority beyond the simple crucifix that hung around his neck and the cardinal's ring that he wore that signified he was the Holy Roman Church's appointed representative in France as assigned by the pope himself. But this particular clergy man's influence and authority went beyond any papal mandate.

He had maneuvered, politicked, built influence and wealth on his way to becoming the defacto ruler of his nation, he was without peer in the realm. A man to fear, who feared nothing or no one. Yet he seemed to fear that lost letter. The one that Marc-Ange was convinced lay on the bed of a stream running through the woodlands of Le Fere.

After the cardinal had failed to reappear for several minutes, the captain considered that he could safely assume he'd been dismissed and left the office. The problem of how to locate and retrieve the lost missive weighed on his mind, along with the prospect of a new career as a dung shoveler. So deep in thought was he that he walked without thinking about a destination, not aware of his surroundings. While his mind contemplated the future, his feet and belly decided to address a more immediate need.

The aroma of roasting meat, and spilled ale mixed with the unmistakable undertones of vomit and piss bought Marc-Ange out of his distraction. He realized at that moment that beyond a stale piece of bread, and a cold cut of boar that was well past its best, on the road back to Paris, he hadn't really eaten since he'd left those accursed woodlands. He needed sustenance.

The inn, conveniently located just outside the barracks wall, was only about half full as it was around mid-morning. Only those returning from patrol in need of food, or those who lived their lives in their cups would be frequenting it at this time of day. Pushing the problem of the missing document to the back of his mind, Marc-Ange crossed the threshold. Inside was gloomy and it took a few seconds for his eyes to adjust to the new light level and search out a table. There was an empty spot towards the back of the establishment. A table for with just two stools by it. Perfect as he didn't want company.

The food, once it arrived, was passable. The inn had never been noted for its culinary delights but it served to sate his hunger. With his plate cleaned the captain sat back, picked up what would be his third tankard of ale for that morning and started to once more contemplate how he should tackle his problem.

Perhaps, he mused, instead of searching for the lost letter at the end of the trail, he should focus his attention on the start of its journey.

"What if someone finds it and reads it?"

"Stay calm, your Majesty." Madame Marie de Chevuse held out her hand, and Anne the Queen of France took it, and gave it a short squeeze. "After all it is just a letter from a sister to her brother. What harm can it do?"

"We are no ordinary brother and sister. If it's found someone will twist even the most innocent of missives into treason."

"Then we must ensure that '*someone*' doesn't find it."

The Queen of France sat at her writing desk, her head in her hands. Had that conversation only taken place a few short days ago. Now her worst fears were being realized. She had been a fool to listen to the pleas of her brother's ambassador, a fool to write the letter, and a fool to trust in Madame de Chevuse's choice of courier. The stupid little man was lost, and so was her future as queen.

She heard the door to her chambers swing open behind her and the young page clear his throat in anticipation of announcing her visitor. Without turning around she quietly greeted him, "Welcome your eminence. What can I do for the first minister today?"

Cardinal Richelieu stepped to her side. "You do me an honor your Majesty suggesting that you may aide me, when it is I who are your humble servant my Queen." He glanced down at her seated figure, her eyes puffy and cheeks red as if recently streaked by tears. "Are you all right, Majesty? You seem troubled."

"Nothing that need concern you my lord. It is but a minor family matter. You are more importantly occupied on matters of state to concern yourself with such trifles."

"If the family your Majesty refers to is your brother, then it is more than a trifle, it is a matter of state, for he is currently..."

"Forgive the interruption, Cardinal," a new voice entered the conversation from the direction of the still open doorway, "but it is the hour for the Queen's afternoon walk in the gardens."

"Madame de Chevuse," he gave a slight nod of the head in her direction, "such a pleasure to see you."

The queen's lady in waiting and chief confident merely smiled, and stood defiantly by the doorway with the queen's cloak draped across her arm.

Richelieu took the hint and strode from the room, as he passed the lady in waiting he muttered, "Remind your lady that her loyalty is to her marriage bed, and she should mark well where France's real enemies lie."

"That man frightens me."

"You are right to fear him, your Majesty," Madame de Chevuse confirmed as she placed the cloak around her mistresses shoulders, "for his agenda is not that of the Pope, nor your husband's, but of his own."

"Yet he claims to love France above all."

"As long as France remains his to play with. He will broke no interference from outside her borders, nor from within."

"He knows of the letter?"

"Yes, Madam. But knowing about the existence of something, and being able to prove that existence can be two very different things."

"There is hope then?"

"There is always hope, my Queen."

"Show me."

The two women had reached a secluded part of the garden and, the queen having already dismissed the footmen assigned to be always close by to attend to any need, they were alone. As they had talked they'd navigated a well worn but informal pathway to an octagonal pagoda whose elevated situation gave the occupants a panoramic view of the palace gardens. They sat on one of the benches with a space between them. Madame de Chevuse extracted a folded folio of paper from under her own cloak, opened it, and spread a map out into the space.

"Show me." Queen Anne once more requested, although this time with a little more hint of excitement in her voice. "Where was he when he went missing?"

"The Cardinal's man reported losing his trail in the wooded area of this region." Madame de Chevuse's finger jabbed at the map.

The queen smiled. "Le Fere. I do believe that those are my lands."

"Indeed they are your Majesty. They are loyal subjects."

"And one in particular."

"He is retired your Majesty."

"Then he should un-retire, his Queen is in need of his help." The queen emitted a soft sigh, "once again."

"He will need to be persuaded. It won't be easy."

"The you need to go and persuade him. After all you are....."

"Madam, I know exactly what I am to him. But I don't think that will make him change his mind."

"I have more faith in you than you do in yourself my dear Marie. He will be delighted to see you."

"Get out!" The Count de le Fere didn't look around to see who had disturbed his moment of tranquility. He heard a muttered apology from behind him, and something about a visitor followed by a shuffling of feet and the door closing behind the retreating servant. The man was a fool; he knew that the count was not receiving visitors. In fact he'd steadfastly refused to receive formal visitors for years. Once he'd come into his title it was if it had become a curse and a prison of his own making. He would see representatives from those who worked his lands and hunted in his woods. He knew those who fished his rivers, and bred his horses. Those who tended the grapevine were always welcome at their count's hall and table. But they needed no invitation to enter his domain. They knew when and where to reach him. Only those from his past life would be introduced as visitors, and of them he wanted no reminders.

Except one.

The gruff isolationist count pulled himself up from his chair. Placed his tankard on the table next to the remnants of a discarded meal, and took stock of himself prior to his nightly rendezvous. He didn't know why he did it for he would no longer impress the ladies as he'd once done, for his stomach had spread, his once proud shoulders slopped, and those fine calfs of his had lost their definition. His other physical attributes that the ladies had once enjoyed had fallen into disuse and he no longer cared. The scars of many battles crisscrossed his frame and his reactions had slowed to the point that he no longer picked up a blade, even to entertain himself with practice. What had happened to him?

The answer lay in the next chamber. The nursery.

Each evening, after he ate, and after the wet nurse had departed, before retiring for the night he would enter the nursery and spend a few tranquil minutes just looking at his sleeping son. He'd never imagined such peace. Being a father had given him a renewed purpose in life. After the tumultuous relationship and violent death of his wife, the secrets that followed, and the things made public that he never wanted to share, he had found solace in wine and a string of women. But in the end it was a drunken night of passion with the mistress of one of his closest friends that had resulted in this miracle.

There'd been no love between them, they both agreed that. It was nothing more than an alcohol fueled encounter, and she had happily given up the child for him to raise as his son.

Raoul was his life now.

He leaned over and lightly kissed the sleeping child on the forehead.

As he bent over the crib he heard the door of the nursery open behind him and a servant cough. "I'm sorry my lord but she insisted."

"He is settled, the wet nurse is no longer needed this evening." He responded without turning around, "Send her back to her chamber."

"It isn't the wet nurse my lord,"

"Then who then dares disturb my son's slumber?"

The answer was one that he had never expected to hear, and the voice was as if from a far away half-remembered dream. Soft and feminine but with undertones of strength and passion. The answer was just two words: "His mother."

Raoul was his life now.

He turned slowly, not wanting to believe what his ears had told him. That she was there. She had promised never to violate this sanctuary, never to call upon their son. Yet here she was. He couldn't help but be transfixed by her. She remained a beauty that stirred passion in him, even though she belonged to another. She wore a travel cloak that was dusty from the road, her face showing a red tinge around the cheeks from the exercise. He wanted to rush to her and hold in his arms once again. The mother of his child.

But he stood his ground, and she stood hers. Keeping a physical distance between them that reflected their unwritten agreement. Until she broke it with a simple gesture and the name he never wanted to hear again.

Madame de Chevuse smiled and held out her hand, "Hello, Athos."

"She is the key to this I'm sure." Captain Marc-Ange paced up and down the small room that he rented above a blacksmith's forge not far from the barracks. It wasn't much, smelt of burning wood, and he was constantly brushing a layer of soot of his clothing in a sisyphean task of futility. But it kept him warm in winter, and it was better than sleeping at the barracks. Here he could think, even above the constant hammering from below.

"But she hasn't been seen for days." The short rotund man who sat on the captain's bed watching him pace responded.

The officer stopped and looked at his Sergeant at Arms. "How would you know about the comings and goings of the queen's favorite?"

He smiled a little sheepishly. "My own sweet Yvette."

"The little strumpet that toils in the royal kitchens by day, and entertains travelers at the inn at night?"

"That's her." The sergeant confirmed, almost bursting with pride. "She knows things."

"So I've heard."

"I meant kitchen gossip. The high and mighty lords and ladies in the palaces and mansions might think that their secrets are safe. But none of them ever notices the serving girl or the footman, but they in turn notice a lot."

"And?"

"And Yvette mentioned that Madame de Chevuse seems to have disappeared from the palace. I reckon the Cardinal has had her seen to."

"Tell me fair Sergeant Jacques Bertillion how you are also privy to the mind of the most powerful man in France."

"Well Yvette told me that Jean, the door page to the queen's private chambers told her that the other day your Madame de Chevuse walked in and interrupted the cardinal when he was in a private conversation with Queen Anne."

Marc-Ange let out a low whistle. "Not the most sensible thing to do."

"Exactly!" exclaimed the sergeant, "And she's not been seen since. So I reckon he had her got rid of."

"So do you think I should ask him at our next meeting?"

The sergeant blanched at the suggestion. "I wasn't suggesting that, sir."

"Maybe I should request an audience with the queen herself and ask her what has become of her closest confident." He smiled, then started pacing again. "So the lady in question has disappeared, that much is certain, even if her fate is not."

"If you don't mind me asking sir, why the interest in the madame if you are after the missing courier?"

"Because the madame engaged him as a courier for the queen's personal messages on a regular basis. The queen trusted her, and she trusted La Porte."

"So if she's disappeared, and you can't ask the cardinal or the queen you need to find someone else she trusts."

Marc-Ange stopped pacing. He turned and stared at his sergeant, then stepped towards the bed and lifted the man on to his feet with an enthusiastic bear hug. "Jacques you are a genius."

Later that evening watching his sergeant's 'Sweet Yvette' ply her trade across the floor of the inn, the captain had to admit she had a certain way about her. She could sweet talk stranger and regular alike, eliciting snippets of information here, bits of gossip there, as well as earning a few sous along the way for the pleasure of her company in the back alley. She would make a remarkable spy, the captain thought, and decided to cultivate her acquaintance, purely for professional purposes, through the sergeant. But that was for a later date.

His quarry this evening sat at the same isolated small table where the captain had broken his fast several days prior. He was sat with his back to the room evidently wanting to be left alone. But he was needed, and Captain Marc-Ange was counting on past encounters to breach the wall of isolation. Gulping down the last dregs of his wine, he rose and threaded his way through the throng towards his target. As he approached the man clearly sensed his presence for he saw the back tense.

Marc-Ange clasped the man on the shoulder in greeting, "Aramis , my friend."

"Go away, cur." The musketeer, did not turn to address him, "I am no friend of yours, moor. Be thankful I have not removed that black hand with my blade."

"Who's there? I know there's someone there. I can hear you moving about." The courier La Porte was frustrated, and nauseated.

The stench of horses was overwhelming, it had been increasingly so since he had first woken up. He had no idea how many days it had been. He turned his head to try and find a more palatable source of fresh air, and immediately wished he hadn't. The pain from his head wound was intense and made him almost wretch. The wound had been roughly treated and bandaged while he was unconscious, but as soon as he had shown signs of stirring a rough hessian sack had been thrown over his head and tied around the neck. He could just make out the difference between night and day plus the occasional blurred shape when someone stepped close. At one point the blade of a dagger ripped a small hole into the sacking and a hollowed out tube of willow pushed through so that he could sup up whatever liquids he was offered, be it water, or soup.

When they were fixing the tube in place they got close enough for him to try and lash out with his feet. That's when he discovered that there was an iron collar around his ankle attached to a sturdy metal chain that led to a hook on the floor. A few times he'd tried to reach up and remove the hood, but his hand was immediately slapped down by what felt like a birch rod. No one had spoken to him, he had no idea where he was, or what was wanted of him. But at least he was alive.

This wasn't the lifestyle he envisaged when he'd been appointed as the queen's courier. He'd imagined leisurely rides in opulent state carriages, traveling between the grand cities of France, stopping at comfortable inns, eating large meals, all on the crown's expense. There might also have been the occasional dashing heroic horse ride to deliver an urgent missive, and he was prepared to endure those as they made for good stories with which to impress the tavern wenches.

The stable, if that's where he was, had gone quiet. He tried again to pull at the hessian sacking. There was no birch rod this time. Instead to his surprise it was a verbal rebuke.

"Keep your hands down," said a rough throaty voice.

"Where am I?"

"None of your concern."

"Who are you?"

"Also none of your concern."

"Then what should I be concerned about?"

"Your life."

"If you were going to kill me you would have slit my throat already, or left me to drown."

"Well aren't you the smart one. We're gonna ransom you. That's a royal household symbol on your coat there. I reckon you must be worth something to someone."

"I'm just a servant, no-one will be bothered about me."

"Maybe not. But that letter you were carrying. That's got to be of interest, seeing who it's addressed to, and whose seal it carries."

"I am not impressed, Ambassador."

"My apologies my liege. It should have arrived by now."

"And yet it has failed to appear. Unless …" King Philip of Spain leant forward in his throne, and bought his face closer to the miserable figure of his ambassador to France quaking before him, "… you have it on your person."

"I followed your Majesty's instructions to the letter. Your sister, Queen Anne of France, was to compose the document you outlined and send it via an independent courier to avoid detection or suspicion." He gulped. "This is what was done." He gulped again, even louder, "Your Majesty." He concluded by hastily making the sign of the cross across his body hoping it might ward off his king's displeasure.

"But it appears that suspicion was aroused, and the plan was detected. What else could explain its disappearance?"

"I know not, my Lord."

"Then my dear Ambassador, I suggest that you find out."

"You look troubled my friend." Colonel Juan Montoya of the king's guard gave the ambassador a hearty slap on the shoulder. His friend ignored it and leant back against the stone wall of the corridor that led to, or in his case from, the throne room.

"Juan, you have no idea."

"Then tell me, and I may come up with one."

"It's quite simple really. Somewhere in the middle of France, the country we recently went to war with in case you'd forgotten, is an unknown courier, carrying a letter to his most gracious Majesty from his sister, who will recall just happens to be queen to our new enemy. If the letter is found and read then our secrets will be revealed, and she will be queen no more."

"Surely the Queen of France, even if she is of our blood, would not commit treason against her own people."

"We would not ask her to do so, but the very fact of the letter may be construed by some as a treasonous act."

"By *some* you mean that retched Cardinal, the true enemy of Spain."

"Exactly."

"I see your conundrum." The colonel smiled, "And I may indeed have an idea. It's been a long time since I visited our friends to the north."

The ambassador stared at his friend, "You're crazy."

"That I may be, but what better time for a crazy man to become a hero, than in a time of war?"

"War, Madame, is a serious business," Louis XIII, the King of France addressed his wife. "France is surrounded on three sides by Spain and her allies, while the English lay claim to the watery channel to the fourth."

"I am well aware of that my husband."

"Yet you are a Hasburg, and it is Hasburgs we face. Your brother, Philip of Spain, lies to my south; he also controls the Dutch territories to my north. While the other Hasburgs and the Holy Roman emperor wait in the east. You, yourself carry the title of Anne of Austria, a Hasburg title, do you not."

"That is true."

"So I must ask myself where do my wife's loyalties lie?"

"With France my King. Did I not celebrate your recent victory against my brother's armies in the north at Les Avins?"

"You did, Madame."

"And do I not provide council on the ways of the Spanish court when asked?"

"That also is true."

"So may I ask why do you question my loyalty to you, my husband, and France, my country?"

"The Cardinal tells me you have been in correspondence with your brother."

"Does the Cardinal have proof of this your Majesty? Has he shown you any such letters? And is it now against your wishes for me to communicate with my brother?"

The king looked at his wife, mixed emotions playing across his face. Concern, love, suspicion, care, and a desire to do the best for his country, and for Anne herself. "Your brother is now the avowed enemy of France," he lowered his voice, "be careful my dear that you do not find yourself in that same position."

Alone in her apartment, Anne, Queen of France fumed with indignation. Richleau had turned her husband against her. It wouldn't be long until he manipulated the masses too. He would make her the most hated woman in France. She'd be branded a traitor and made the scapegoat for anything the Hasburgs did. She needed that letter back. But her courier, La Porte, was missing; her confidant was absent on a mission to recruit a most reluctant ally to her cause. But she couldn't wait.

She needed help, now, right here in Paris.

Suddenly a thought struck her, if the Count de le Fere was proving to be a reluctant ally; maybe his former companions would be more open to her pleas. She hastily scribbled a note and handed it to the page standing patiently in the corner of the room. The two gold coins she placed in his hand an inducement to ensure that it would be delivered to the right place.

"Excuse me," the young page nervously tugged on the skirts of the serving wench. It took several repeated tugs before he succeeded in catching her attention.

"What are you after, my little Lord." Yvette smiled and patted the page on the head, "Lost your way?"

"I'm here on the Queen's business." The page straightened his back and stuck his chest out to signify the importance of his errand. "I am searching for a famous hero."

"Aren't we all my dear." Yvette let out a raucous laugh impressed at her own humor.

"Do you know the whereabouts of the Chevalier d'Herblay?" the young man continued. He had been told not to return to the palace until the note had been placed in the hand of the man whose formal title graced the cover, a title inscribed by the queen's own hand.

Yvette continued to laugh, "I do not, for surely if a man of such grandeur ever passed over the threshold into this dung heap, I'd make sure I knew about it, and make sure I knew him too." She nudged the page. "Oh, I'd know him." She sighed and stopped laughing. "But my fortune doesn't run to opportunities such as being on intimate terms with the chevalier you seek."

The page also sighed and dropped his chin in resignation, "Then my mission is a failure, for I was informed that the man I seek is known to frequent this establishment."

"Indeed he does."

The page felt a strong grip across the top of his shoulder by the edge of his neck. He winced slightly in pain, and glanced down to see the dusky tones of the hand that held him. The page twisted and looked up into a smiling, slightly amused face, of a man in the uniform of the cardinal's guard.

"I know you, sir." The young page pulled himself straight, feeling somewhat emboldened. "You are Captain Marc-Ange, the moor."

"That I am." The officer bowed.

"You are in the Cardinal's service."

Marc-Ange waved his hand in front of himself with a downward motion to encompass his clothes. "So the uniform would suggest."

"Then, sir, you are no friend to my lady, The Queen."

"That is an erroneous assumption my young friend."

The page spat at the captain's feet. "I doubt that. In any case you are certainly not the man I seek. You are not the Chevalier d'Herblay."

"No I am not, nor did I ever lay claim to his name or title." Marc-Ange smiled, "But I do know where to find him."

"Where?" The page's voice rose in pitch with his excitement.

"He awaits your queen's command," Marc-Ange pointed to the far side of the tavern, "under that table over there."

Yvette once again burst into peels of laughter. She also pointed at the recumbent form sprawled among the straw and scraps of the tavern floor, a snore of thunderous proportions emanating from its general direction. "That! That is your famous hero? That drunken sot is no brave chevalier. That's the musketeer, Aramis."

Marc-Ange strode towards the drunken figure on the floor. He kicked the sole of the man's boot. "Exactly," he turned to the confused page, "deliver your lady's message, and I pray that this time he will listen."

Aramis placed the note face down on the table, and shook his head once again with the dual aim of trying to clear his thoughts, and shake of the scummy water from the horse trough that had been deposited over his head in order to revive him from his sodden stupor. "Your lady asks too much of me." He snarled at the young page cowering across the table.

"She asks for your loyalty and protection," the boy answered with a quavering voice, "you have provided as much before I am told."

"Who told you that?"

"He did." The page tipped his head back to indicate the man stood behind him.

"She will always have my loyalty, but my protection is less certain these days."

Captain Marc-Ange stepped around from behind the boy, and as he drew alongside swiftly pulled the dagger from his belt and held it against the page's neck.

Yvette screamed.

Shaking off the last vestiges of his hangover the musketeer leapt to his feet pushing his stool backwards and swiping the table to one side. The queen's written plea slid unnoticed into the straw and rushes. A sword was in his hand in an instant, its blade raised and pointed at the chest of the cardinal's guard. "Let the boy go, or I'll run you through you black blaggard"

Marc-Ange pushed the boy to one side, dropped the dagger to the floor and started to move his arms upward in a gesture of capitulation. As his hands passed his belt a quick flick of the wrist and his sword was drawn smoothly and quickly and now bridged the gap between himself and Aramis. The swords touched blades but neither wavered.

"Now you show your true colors, Ange. Once a cardinal's man, always a cardinal's man."

Marc-Ange did not say a word. His eyes remained locked on those of the musketeer.

"Please," Yvette squeaked, "not in here."

Neither man responded.

To the young page the stand off seemed to last an interminable length, yet it was probably only a few seconds. He didn't know who moved first, but suddenly both blades were a cascade of motion. Thrusts and parries; feints, attacks, and blocks. It was difficult to keep track of. Neither man moved from his position, neither gained or lost an inch. This was more of a martial ballet than a fight.

Then just as suddenly as it had started, it finished.

In the middle of a defensive move, Marc-Ange dropped the tip of his sword leaving himself open to attack. The sudden lack of resistance against his blade caused Aramis to take an involuntary step forward and he only just managed to redirect his blade so it didn't pierce his opponent in the chest.

"Why did you drop your guard?" Aramis growled. "I could have killed you."

"But you didn't." He nodded in the direction of the page, "and despite what you believe about yourself you are still protective of the queen, or her servants at least."

Aramis scowled and looked at the boy, "Tell your lady I accept her commission."

René Laver considered himself to be something like a leaf on the wind. No matter which way the prevailing political storms blew from Paris, he would let them wash over him. This way he had kept his small inn on the edge of the Le Fere region in business for many years. It had become a safe haven on the road for travelers of all sorts. Laver never asked questions as long as a traveler had enough coinage in their pocket to cover the cost of any ale supped or food eaten. It had also become an unwritten rule that in Laver's tavern no-one else asked questions of their fellow travelers either.

Which is why he was now suspicious of the man who currently sat at one of his tables enjoying a roast leg of mutton and a tankard of ale. The man's cloak, while filthy with mud and dust from the road, was clearly well cut and from a fine cloth. Yet it bore no insignia or patterns which might signify the wearer's allegiances. His hat was similarly of fine quality if a little battered from the effects of several days rain. But the most suspicious thing was the fact that the stranger was charming and talkative. He seemed to find it easy to engage anyone who passed his table in lively conversation during which he revealed nothing, but somehow others told him the stories of their travels and troubles. And then there was the way he spoke french. It was too perfect. As if it had been taught by those who knew the mechanics of the language rather than learned by living it.

Laver watched the stranger over the course of several hours. The man appeared to eat and drink steadily, but he took only token bites and occasional sips of his ale. Just enough to appear sociable to those who he invited to join him, but not enough to dull his senses or slow his wits. Those he invited to join him were mainly woodsmen, and hunters. His expression seemed fixed in a shallow welcoming smile but his eyes betrayed a steely determination. People came and went from his table, but none of the

"Why did you drop your guard?"

stories he heard appeared to satisfy him. Whatever, or whoever, he was looking for was not to be found. Eventually the stranger shouted for his tankard to be refreshed.

René Laver intercepted the serving girl, and took the tankard from her hand, before marching over to the stranger and thumping it down on the roughly hewn table in front of him.

"You ask too many questions my friend."

"I am not your friend," the stranger grumbled, "and my conversation is my business."

"It looks to me like you're anxious to make a lot of friends."

"As I said it is none of your business what I do and who I talk to."

"If it takes place in my inn, then I consider it my business."

"If this is your place, then you need to be more considerate of your guests."

"I suggest that you, sir, have exceeded your time as my 'guest,' and that you depart immediately."

"*Sinverguenza!*" With the curse still fresh on his lips the stranger pushed his chair back and stood up, his hand flying to the hilt of his sword. "You test my patience innkeeper."

René Lavar stared at the man stood before him, "My God, you are a Span..." He never finished his declaration as the sword was drawn and thrust into the luckless man's belly.

"If you wish to know innkeeper," the stranger whispered over the fallen man," You died on the sword of Colonel Juan Montoya, loyal servant of his majesty, King Philip of Spain. And soon your country will die with you."

As his life ebbed away from him, Lavar watched his assailant stride to the door of the inn, there to be greeted by a man in what looked to be the uniform of the cardinal's guard. René Lavar did not know what treachery he had just witnessed, but it didn't matter for he was now beyond any mortal cares.

La Porte had given up caring about his fate. He knew he was going to die, even if the time, place, or method was still unknown to him. He would either be drugged, his throat slit while he slept, or thrown in the nearby river. He was certain of it. Which made the sudden light as his hood was removed less of a shock and more of a moment of internal reflection. This was it, he knew, his last moments were upon him.

"What do you know of the Spaniard?" The voice was rough and demanding.

LaPorte tried to respond, but he hadn't spoken to anyone in days, his throat was parched dry, so all he emitted was a squeak.

"Water." The rough voiced questioner barked. "And I ask again, what do you know of the Spaniard?"

La Porte blinked to help speed up the adjustment of his eyes to the new light level. As he did so a tumbler of water was placed in his hands. He gulped its contents down, and choked on the sudden onrush of liquid. It was the first time he'd consumed anything other than via the willow tube in what felt like weeks. As he spluttered he croaked, "What Spaniard?"

"Colonel Juan Montoya."

La Porte's eyes had adjusted, and he squinted up to take in the man who stood over him. A tall man who stooped a little, and showed signs of good soft living, although his bearing hinted at him having been something else in his earlier days, a soldier perhaps. "I know no Spaniards," La Porte answered, a hint of defiance in his voice.

"Yet I am told that you carried a document intended for the eyes of the King of Spain."

"I will not discuss the details of my mission with the likes of you." La Porte used what little moisture he had accumulated in his mouth to summon up some spittle which he ejected at the feet of the man.

The small act of defiance was ignored.

The man turned and walked out of the horse stables that had served as La Porte's prison. He stopped at the threshold, turned back and gestured at La Porte. "Unchain him, clean him up, and send him to me. We will find the truth."

La Porte felt a shiver run through him. The certainty of death was now under question; his fate unknown. That worried him more than imminent death ever had.

"If he knows I'm here with you, he'll have me killed." Marie de Chevuse looked across the table at Athos. It was clear that he was still annoyed by her presence. He'd listened to her tale as she pleaded the queen's case to the former musketeer, but he had seemed unmoved. His expression had not changed, except for perhaps a momentary scowl when the cardinal's name had been invoked. But in general the father of her son had remained grumpily stoic. "Are you going to remain silent throughout my stay here?"

He raised his head from looking down at the plate of meat that lay before him and for the first time since her arrival looked her directly in the eyes. "You will not be staying here." He waved his arm in a circle to indicate his home. "There is an inn in the village nearby where you will be comfortable."

She shuddered. "The one where the innkeeper was murdered? I think not."

"What you think is of no concern to me. Stay there, or return to Paris. It matters not."

"I cannot return to my queen without news of you agreeing to her commission. I will not fail her."

"You already have, for I have no interest in involving myself in her affairs again."

Marie ignored the harsh admonishment, "And the inn isn't safe, what if the murderer returns."

"The Spaniard is far away from here by now."

"What Spaniard?" Marie's interest was piqued by this piece of information.

"The man who killed Lavar." Athos responded, with the first traces of interest she'd heard in his voice since her arrival, "Colonel Juan Montoya."

"How do you know his name?" She asked.

Athos broke a piece of bread off the nearby loaf and dipped it in the gravy on his plate, picking up the juice in a sweeping motion. It seemed as if his body was waking up as muscle memory started to kick in. He gestured with the dripping bread almost as if pointing with his long ignored blade, "In his arrogance he whispered his name and allegiance to the dying man. He must of thought that it was low enough that none around would her. But Claudette, the serving wench was stood close enough, and she heard every word."

"So you are going to let this Spaniard insult you?"

Athos grabbed his wine, drained the cup and stared across the table at his unwanted guest with a quizzical expression on his face.

"He murders one of your tenants, and not just any tenant, but your trusted innkeeper. And you do nothing. He is an enemy of your country. And you do nothing. He is a threat to your queen. And you do nothing." Marie de Chevuse let her voice rise with each accusation. Pushing her chair back she rose, with a glass of wine clasped in her hand. She stared at Athos as she gulped a mouthful down in a manner rarely seen from ladies of the court. Looking down at the remains of the wine in the glass, she sighed as if in resignation, then with a sudden flick of her wrist sent the remnants of her drink flying across the table towards the count. Athos, while caught unawares, still retained enough of his inherent reflexes to lean backwards so that the liquid landed in his lap rather than his face.

"A waste of good wine, my dear Marie."

"If that is the case then your appreciation of fine wines has declined, Athos, as I would rank it mediocre at best. And the question remains my lord of the damp crotch. You still intend to do nothing?"

Athos grabbed a table napkin and started to wipe away at the stains on his clothes. Without looking up from his task he responded. "Madame. I have already done more than nothing." With that he reached for the small hand bell that sat upon the table used for summoning servants to his side. It emitted a light trill that Marie doubted could be heard more than a few meters away and yet even before the reverberations died out a member of the household staff appeared.

"Bring our other guest to join us."

" Yes, my lord." The servant hesitated, "Which one?"

"What do you mean which one?"

Before the servant could answer, the door to the dining room flew open with a flourish, and three figures made their dramatic entrance. The central figure was the short disheveled courier, flanked on either side by men of military bearing and authority, one wearing the uniform of a member of Richleau's guard, the other that of a king's musketeer.

"La Porte!" Madame de Chevuse gasped, shortly followed by a more modulated "Ara...."

The name died in her throat as she caught sight of Athos, who had remained silent at the intrusion. Almost before the figures had crossed the room's threshold his hand had flown to his side where his sword would normally have hung. Muscle memory and instinct took over, the instant the his hand grasped empty air it kept moving and swept across the table top picking up a sharp carving knife as it went. In a smooth continuous movement the knife flew in a lethal arc towards the newcomer in the Cardinal's colors. While Athos may have been without his sword, others weren't, and a flash of steel blade intercepted the projectile before it struck home. The knife fell uselessly to the floor with a dull thud that punctuated the now silent tableau. Five people looked at each other in a mix of confusion and fear. Athos strode towards his intended victim, and stopped just short of an arm's length away. He jabbed his hand into the man's chest but his head was turned towards the musketeer with the sword in his hand. "What are you doing here, with him?"

The question went unanswered as the musketeer gesticulated with his sword in the direction of the queen's lady, "What are you doing here, with her?"

"She is the mother of my child."

"You both swore to have nothing to do with each other after she handed over the boy to you. You dishonor me for a second time when I may have been ready to call you 'friend' once again. I demand satisfaction."

Athos shrugged and gave a wry smile, "As you see my dear Aramis, I have no sword and even you won't attack an unarmed man when it's a question of honor."

"Don't tempt me," came the low growl of a response. "Arm your self, Count." The use of the title sounded almost like an insult.

"Allow me." The cardinal's man stepped forward. His drawn sword lay with its blade flat across the top of his crooked arm, the pommel pointing outward towards Athos.

"Stay out of this Marc-Ange," Aramis hissed.

"And miss the opportunity to watch two masters in action? I think not. The offer stands."

Arthos slowly reached for the proffered sword. "I will deal with the presence of a member of the cardinal's guard within my walls shortly." Having pulled the sword away from Marc-Ange's arm, he hefted the blade in his hand testing its feel and balance. It was a fine weapon, perhaps not the match of his own, but it would suffice in the circumstances. "Now, Aramis I suggest you withdraw the veiled accusation behind Marie's presence here, and come to your senses before I test the efficiency of your companion's blade."

Aramis leaped at his fellow musketeer. His sword was met at the top of its arc by Athos's borrowed one. The blades slid along each other until both met the resistance of the hand guards. The interlocked weapons were pulled apart and each man took a step back to size up his opponent. Athos felt the edge of the dining hall table in the small of his back as Aramis once again lunged toward him. He twisted and rolled to one side as his opponent's blade struck the table, leaving a groove and raising a shower of splinters. Athos was stunned by the apparent ferocity of the attack. He and Aramis had had their disagreements before, even crossed swords a few times during their long, if somewhat contentious friendship and those encounters had always been more on the level of a sparring match. But the groove in his table was a physical indication that his one-time companion was in deadly earnest, with the emphasis on deadly. On the other hand Athos had been pleasantly surprised at his own reflexes and the speed with which he had dodged the blow. Instinct and muscle memory had kicked in. As he rolled away he realized that Aramis had overreached himself, and quickly struck his off balance opponent across the back with the flat of his blade. Aramis roared, and twisted to meet his adversary who now stood with a chair between them using the chair back as an impromptu shield. Aramis leapt at the chair planting his right foot on the seat and pushing up; as he rose we swept his sword arm downwards only to meet empty air. Athos had once again side stepped the intended blow. Landing on his feet, Aramis swept the room to see Athos stood in the open space at the center beckoning his opponent to come join him. The two met in a flourish of swords. To the onlooking Marc-Ange it seemed as if a tornado had arisen in that dining room, but as he looked closer he began to realize that the tornado was Aramis, while the calm eye of the storm was a hardly moving Athos.

"That's enough." The commanding voice of Marie de Chevuse carried across the chamber.

The two combatants dropped their sword points, while maintaining a wary eye on each other.

"Neither of you will win. You know that. And I won't be the subject of your stupid squabbles anymore. I make my own decisions, and I go where I will. No one commands me except for my queen." She pointed in the direction of the disheveled courier still standing in the doorway unsure of what he had seen, or his own fate. "As such I demand to know why La Porte is here, and in such condition."

The courier entered the room and stood before the queen's confidante. He was nervous, not only of her, but of the men in the room. "Madame, forgive me, for I have failed both you and our mistress the queen." He glanced suspiciously at the cardinal's man. "I was hunted by this man. He even set his dogs after me." La Porte shuddered at the recollection. "I fell and was rendered senseless. On my awakening I was bound and chained, kept in seclusion and darkness."

Athos laughed. "I'd say you were kept in a stable. For that is where you were found."

"What of the package you were entrusted with?" This time the voice belonged to the former hunter.

"I will never tell you." He spat in Marc-Ange's direction.

"Then perhaps you will tell me?" The lady's voice was calm and soothing as she took the courier's shaking hand. She looked into his eyes.

Watching the tableau the two musketeers smiled at each other in mutual recognition, both knew what it was like to succumb to that particular gaze.

La Porte hung his head in shame. "I have no idea as to its fate Madame. My captors told me they had removed it and were seeking to sell it to whoever may pay a good price."

"Did you know your captors?" Again the cardinal's man spoke.

La Porte shook his head. "My head was always covered. I never saw them; I saw no-one until this man rescued me." He nodded in Athos's direction. But I did notice that whenever the leader of the kidnappers leant close to me he smelled heavily of beer and tobacco."

"*Merde.*" Athos swore. "Lavar."

"So the Spaniard has it." Marie muttered, "For he killed Lavar."

"We don't know that for sure," Athos countered. "I mean we know he killed Lavar, we don't know if he has the queen's document."

"What Spaniard?" Aramis and Marc-Ange asked in unison.

"Lavar was a poor innkeeper at best," Athos looked around the main room of the inn with disgust, "but without even his meager administrations it has fallen into even lower levels of disrepute than I thought possible." The room was just as crowded as usual but now it smelled even ranker than usual of ale, vomit, piss, and shit. It appeared that the rushes covering the floor had not been cleared and changed since the former proprietor's demise for they could be seen to move where vermin skittered among them looking for scraps. The cooking smells that had once masked the odor of unwashed humanity with aroma of roasting meat and fresh baked bread now instead delivered the promise of a greasy stew and burnt offerings. The clients had also seemed to have sunk lower, with fewer travelers and more cut-throats and highway robbers, all served by an increased number of salacious wenches. "Where is Claudette?" Athos raised his voice above the din of the room.

"What is it to you?" A large mass of solid muscle detached itself from the nearest table and stood before Athos. He was at least a head taller and broad across the shoulders. He pushed up his sleeves to expose well developed arms covered in rough tattoos that Athos recognized as the sign of a particularly vicious gang of thieves that he believed had been driven out of the Le Fere woods.

"I am the Count de Fere, and these are my lands. This inn is under my protection, as are the roads, woods, and the people of this region." Athos drew his sword and in a swift single motion brought it up so the point lay in the centre of the thief's chest. "You and your cut throats are not welcome here. You will leave. But first tell me of the whereabouts of Claudette."

The large man placed the palm of his hand against the blade point and casually pushed it away. "And I am the Count of the Road and these" he waved his arm to indicate the crowd behind him, "are the people under my protection." The pronouncement was met with raucous laughter from his compatriots. "I have no knowledge of the wench you named, for she is not one of us. As for this inn, since the passing of Lavar, it is now under my protection too. I therefore suggest that you depart, my dear Count." He bowed towards Athos in what was clearly a mocking gesture. Every man in the inn stood as if the bow had been a signal, and a variety of blades of different sizes and quality appeared in their hands.

"It appears that you have a disagreement to sort out." The gruff voice of Aramis spoke from behind as he and Marc-Ange stepped through the doorway.

The self-proclaimed Count of the Road, took in the new arrivals. "I have no quarrel with the king's musketeers nor the cardinal's men."

"If you pick a fight with the Count, then we are part of the package I'm afraid."

"You are vastly outnumbered, Musketeer, my twenty against you three."

"Is that your idea of honor, thief?" Athos sneered. "Face me alone."

"Athos," Aramis interjected, "He isn't worth your time."

Athos turned to his friend to provide a counter point to this observation. It was a move indicative of his recent inactivity, for it was a serious error. As soon as Athos's gaze moved away, the thief rushed his opponent. The impact drove the breath from Athos and he staggered backward a few steps. Pressing his advantage the thief threw his arms around Athos pinning the count's arms to his side. As he squeezed Athos reflexively loosened his grip on the handle of his sword and it fell to the floor with a clatter. One of the other thieves made to retrieve it, but Marc-Ange stepped forward and put his foot on the blade. He looked at the opportunist thief and simply shook his head. The man stepped back. All focus in the room was now on the two men locked in mutual combat.

His movements severely restricted by the grip he was held in Athos used the only weapon available to him, his head. He sunk his neck down into his shoulders as far as possible, the suddenly drove his head upwards with

"I have no quarrel with the King's musketeers..."

as much force as he could muster smashing the crown of his skull into the base of the jaw of the bigger man. At the same time he scrapped the side of his right boot down the shin of the man's left leg. Both men were left dazed by the impact and staggered apart. Athos only had a headache to deal with while his opponent was reeling from the impact to his jaw and the pain in his leg. Shaking his head and limping, he once again rushed at Athos. This time the count kept his eye on his opponent, and as the man lunged he used the advantage of two good legs and his agility to dash around one of the inn tables, placing it between himself and his fellow combatant. As he circled the table he grabbed at one of the pewter tankards that sat on its surface. The larger man took a deep breath and roared to clear his head of the pain. As he did so he grabbed the table and swept it to one side. Athos took two steps back, pulled back his arm and pitched the tankard. It hit the thief squarely between the eyes. The man stopped mid roar, and with an expression that seem to mix confusion, surprise, and pain, slid unconscious into the rancid layer of rushes covering the inn floor.

"Take your man, and leave these lands." Marc-Ange announced in a stern loud voice, "Remember they are under the protection of the Count de Le Fere," He paused and looked at Aramis, "and his companions."

The thieves scrambled from their various positions around the inn, and made a hasty retreat for the door. Six of them carrying the supine body of their leader with them.

Aramis let out a hearty laugh, "You have an over developed sense of the dramatic for a captain of the cardinal's guard, my moorish friend."

"We still need to find Claudette," Athos staggered as the adrenaline rush of the fight subsided. He suddenly sat down on the floor, "and I need a drink."

"I think both needs have just been answered," Aramis pointed towards a door at the back of the inn as a scared looking young woman, cautiously entered carrying three overflowing tankards.

"Are you sure he didn't give anything to the Spaniard?"

"As sure as I can be of anything, my lord. It all happened so quick. They was talking, then they was arguing, and next thing I saw that Spaniard was sticking his sword in René."

"And that was all you saw?"

"No my lord, as he left the Spaniard was greeted at the door by a man dressed like him." And with that pronouncement, she pointed at Marc-Ange.

"This gets more complex by the minute." Athos turned to the cardinal's man, "What do you know of this?"

"Nothing beyond which I was tasked to do. Recover the letter."

"Is that what you're looking for?" The serving girl asked. "That cursed letter. There's been nothing but trouble and grief since René turned up with that thing claiming it would make him rich, and once he'd sorted things out he'd take me to Paris and we'd buy a proper coach inn instead of this dump." She caught herself, "Sorry, Count. No offense intended."

Athos brushed the apology aside, "You know where the letter is?"

"He gave it to me for safe keeping. Do you want me to get it?"

Three voices responded in unison. "Yes."

The battered, torn, and water damaged missive sat on dining room table in the Count de le Fere's castle. Around the table stood the count, the musketeer, the cardinal's captain, the queen's courier, and the lady-in-waiting.

"What happens now?" The courier asked.

The count picked up the letter, "It seems that Madame de Chevuse and I must commit treason."

"I should have you arrested just for standing there. You are, after all, an enemy of France." Cardinal Richelieu leant across the expanse of his mahogany desk, lowered his voice. "In fact I could have you killed. So tell me why I shouldn't."

"Because, your eminence, while our countries maybe in conflict, you and I wish the same goal. The utter humiliation and disgrace of Anne of Austria."

"Why should I wish ill to the Queen of France?"

"I notice you use your words carefully Cardinal." The visitor smiled. "She may be the 'Queen of France' as you term it, but I believe to you she is simply the wife to your King, and possibly a Hasburg spy. While to me she is a distraction for my lord, her brother, and a potential French spy." He bowed in the cardinal's direction, "If you will forgive my impertinence."

"I will not dignify your supposition with an answer," The cardinal paused, and stared across the table at the other mine. Silence pervaded the office for several seconds as they took measure of each other. The cardinal smiled, sat

Alan J. Porter

down, and gestured for his visitor to also sit. "So, tell me Colonel Montoya, how do you propose to remove our mutual problem?"

Three figures riding full speed on horseback across the French country-side. Riders on a mission. Riders with a purpose.

Athos smiled to himself as the memories came flooding back. Himself and his boon companions heading into danger and intrigue. The drum of hoof beats beating out the promise of adventure for the three musketeers.

A cry from the lead rider bought him out of his reverie. The two fig-ures in front of him weren't Aramis and Porthos, but Marie de Chevuse and the courier known as LaPorte. They were all coated in dust and grime from many days on the road, a fact that LaPorte constantly complained about, as they headed south. Far from the forests of Le Frere or the streets of Paris the lone musketeer was feeling uncertain of his surroundings and had reluctantly relinquished the task of guiding their party to the cou-rier, who claimed to be well acquainted with the road they sought. It was LaPorte's exclamation that had interrupted Athos' memories, and he was none too happy about it. "Why have we stopped?"

"Our destination is over the ridge ahead."

"So, let us be on our way."

"In our current state we would not be taken seriously as representatives of her majesty. The gates would remain closed and our journey would be for naught."

"He has a point." Marie concurred.

"If he doesn't suggest a plan then he will have a point for certain. The point of my sword at his throat."

"There is an inn I know an hour's ride away. We can wash, rest, and change clothes there before we venture into the city."

To his credit the inn was exactly where La Porte had indicated where it would be. His arrival was treated with an exuberant greeting from the landlord, and a squeal of delight from one of the serving girls. Athos was beginning to appreciate just how far the royal courier's influence spread. The inn keeper was equally impressed when LaPorte introduced his com-panions using their titles.

"My Lord, and Lady, how may we serve you?" He bowed obsequiously.

La Porte answered with the request for food, water, and lodgings and they were quickly ushered inside. As was his habit Athos scanned the room as the hastened across the inn interior enroute to the set of stairs at the rear that lead to the few private rooms available. The majority of the patrons looked to be the locals he expected, but in a far corner two broad shouldered figures sat hunched over a table apparently deep in conversation. Athos's gaze and sweep of the room, nor his progress, faltered at the sight of the men, but he had noted their presence.

"Did you see them?" Marie asked as they entered the room.

"Yes."

"How did they know we'd be here?"

"It doesn't matter now. We stick to the plan."

The following morning, refreshed and suitably attired in cleaner clothes the three returned to the ridge from which they had detoured. This time they rode on. As they crested the rise in the road Athos got his first sight of the walls of Toulouse. He was impressed. The capital of the Occitanie region was still surrounded by its sturdy Roman walls, and the sun light highlighted the terra coat bricks of its buildings, producing the pinkish hue that gave the city the name of La Ville Rose. It was a beautiful sight and should have been one of the jewels of France. But there was a problem. For the city that lay in front of them stood too close to the Spanish border for the musketeer's comfort.

"Come." La Porte gestured down the road in the direction of the city gates.

"I don't like this." Athos cautioned.

Madame de Chevuse sniggered. "Ah, the mighty hero quakes in his boots."

Athos bristled at the rebuke, "I am just being cautious. We are too close to enemy territory. Who knows what awaits us beyond those walls."

"It is still France beyond this walls my dear Athos," Marie responded, "and we are on the queen's business." And with that she spurred her horse forward and galloped towards the city leaving the courier and the musketeer in her wake.

"I suppose we should ride after her." La Porte shrugged.

The gates of the city swung open to greet the riders, and having caught up with their charge Athos and La Porte entered in line astern of Madame de Cheveuse. Athos scanned his surroundings as they rode deeper into the city. All seemed normal as the citizens passed by on their business, and various merchants plied their trade. Yet there was something that didn't seem right to the musketeer. His battle tuned senses had never let him down, and while he was somewhat out of practice he still relied on his intuition.

"No one is looking at us," Athos suddenly remarked.

"What do you mean?" La Porte responded

"We are three strangers in this city, and no-one has even glanced in our direction as we rode by. That's not right. It's like they've been instructed to ignore us."

"Who could do that?" Marie asked with a disbelieving lilt in her voice. "And more importantly, why would they?"

"So no matter who may be asked, they can say, truthfully, that they never saw us in the city."

"Your imagination is getting the better of you Athos," Marie laughed.

The three riders rode on in silence for several more minutes, but Athos' words started to hang heavy on their minds as his companions noticed the citizens' apparent indifference to their passing. As they rode deeper into the city they also observed that the number of citizens in the streets noticeably thinned out until they were all alone. An unnatural silence fell around them as the only sound became that of their own horses' hooves striking the cobble stones of the major thoroughfare.

The street eventually opened up to the extensive plaza of the Place du Capitale, its environs also devoid of life. Or at least that's how it seemed on first impression.

"There," La Porte gestured across the plaza towards the magnificent facade of the regional capital building that dominated the far side of the open space. The figure of a man could just be seen stood outside an iron gateway.

"Wait." La Porte raised his hand in a gesture to tell his companions to bring their mounts to a halt. "Whoever that is, they are stood right in front of the entrance to the courtyard of Henri IV."

"Why is that important?" Marie asked.

"He's sending a message." La Porte responded.

"Who?"

"Richelieu." Athos hissed.

"Exactly," La Porte confirmed. "Three years ago the rebellious Duke de Montmorency was executed on that very spot." The courier paused, and slowly looked at each of his companions in turn, "On the explicit orders of the Cardinal."

"He's letting us know that even this close to the Spanish border, he is in control of the citizens of France. He has played us like chess pieces."

"We'll I'm in no mood to be treated like a mere pawn, nor to wait for his next move." Athos' hand dropped to his side and swiftly drew his sword.

With blade raised he spurred his horse forward towards the cardinal's messenger. He rode with rage and little thought. He did not know the man he rode towards, his presence on this spot was enough. The musketeer had been pulled out of his retirement against his wishes, left his precious son behind, dragged across the country driven by duty and obligation. This was where it would stop. As he approached the figure his sword arm poised ready to slash down. Just as the arm tensed and started its downward arc, Athos glanced in the direction of his target mentally tracking his blades path, and looked straight into the eyes of Aramis.

The blade swung.

It took all of Athos' skill, reflexes, and coordination to reign in his horse and alter the path of his sword. Even so its tip sliced along the sleeve of his friend rending material but thankfully missing the flesh beneath.

Aramis didn't move or flinch under the assault.

Athos leapt from his now stationary horse, and ran to his fellow musketeer grabbing him by the shoulders. "My God, I could have killed you. Why are you here? This was not our plan. I took you for one of Richelieu's messengers."

Aramis slowly shook his head in resignation, "That is the role that has been forced upon me my friend. And the Cardinal demands that you turn over the Queen's letter to his representatives."

"Your jest is in poor taste."

"Unfortunately I do not jest." Aramis leaned his head backward as into gesture behind him towards the capital building, "nor am I alone."

Athos peered past his friend straining to pierce the gloom of the shadows in front of the building. A glint of light off metal focused his attention. The barrel of a single musket was aimed in their direction. "Primed?"

"Of course."

"Tricky. And your role in this tableau?"

"Sacrificial lamb."

For the first time Athos realized that his friend had neither moved nor gestured during their exchange. A glance down revealed a tight coil of rope encircling Aramis' ankles. From it a rope ran vertically up to a similar cuff of rope around the musketeer's wrists. The bound man had been placed in the plaza as bait. Athos cursed to himself as he realized that he and his two companions had ridden into a trap.

Athos spun on his heels and shouted back at LaPorte and Marie, but the words died on his lips. Ranged out behind them were a dozen of the cardinal's guards in a semi circle that tightened as they approached. The courier and the queen's lady dismounted, drew swords and faced the approaching threat.

"There is no need for bloodshed," a voice announced out of the shadows, "after all I believe we all want the same thing, for the queen's letter to be handed off to a representative of the Spanish court. And what am I, if not that?" Colonel Juan Montoya stepped out of the shadows, and alongside him stepped Captain Marc-Ange of the cardinal's guard.

"You clam to represent the Spanish court, yet here you stand alongside Richelieu's man." Athos tried to keep reason in his voice as he hid his anger. He had accepted Marc-Ange into his home on good faith at the word of a friend who had now also been betrayed. He failed. "Are we not at war?" he growled.

"Politics and ambition make strange bedfellows, Musketeer." The Spaniard smiled. "The Cardinal wishes to remove this troublesome foreign Queen from France. The proof of a letter from her to her brother, my King, would, irrespective of its actual content, be tantamount to treason, as I believe you well know as your intention was to honor your Queen's wishes and deliver it aware of the potential consequences if discovered. The Cardinal would brand your mistress a traitor and dishonor her name. As for me, I intend to see his plan realized."

"What do you gain, from such an action?"

"What every soldier craves. Honor and glory. For branding Anne of Austria a traitor would be an insult to the honor of Spain and the Habsburgs. An insult not to be tolerated. Enough of an insult for me to lead an army across our common border, an action that has so far been denied me."

"Your King approves of this plan?"

"He is ignorant of it. And will remain so until my moment of triumph."

"Yet to achieve this triumph, you consort with your worst enemy." Athos nodded in the direction of Captain Marc-Ange of the cardinal's guard stood beside the Spaniard.

"War makes strange bedfellows, my dear Count."

"And you, Captain of the guard," he looked straight at Marc-Ange with barely concealed distaste, "I allowed you in my home, and you repay me by standing with an enemy of France. What is your role in all this?"

"To protect my Sovereign by rooting out traitors." As he finished his proclamation, Marc-Angie's sword blade was drawn, its tip pointed at Athos, "and now Musketeer, it is time for those who would disrespect the crown to pay the price."

Marie de Cheveuse's scream echoed around the Place du Capitale as she saw Marc-Angie's sword strike towards the defenseless back of her long-term lover, Aramis. What folly had led to this moment?

Unseen by the grieving woman the sword did not strike flesh; instead it bit deep into the musketeer's bonds, slicing through ropes. With a quick shake of his shoulders the ropes dropped from around his arms and he quickly bent down and pulled them from his ankles. Straightening up Aramis raised his arm in perfect time to catch the hilt of the same weapon that had freed him from captivity. Captain Marc-Ange had thrown the sword into the air; while it flew away he drew a second weapon from his belt. The captain and the musketeer now stood back to back swords drawn against a common enemy.

"The Sovereign I serve is my Queen, and your treacherous plans are now known Montoya." Marc-Ange shouted. "Be prepared to stand against us, and meet justice."

Montoya laughed. "Captain I believe you to be outnumbered and out-classed." He gave a wave of his hand, a signal for a dozen men stepped from the shadows to surround the small group.

"You have some interesting companions," Athos noted. "I see several of the cardinal's guards that I recognize , and I assume from their dress the others must be a small sampling of your Spanish men-at-arms? No matter, who they be, or their numbers, they stand against Musketeers, and we will not be divided."

"I see only two musketeer's."

"True only two of us bear that distinction, but our companions, the captain, the courier, and even the formidable lady, have the makings of musketeers, and we are proud to stand shoulder to shoulder with them."

"So be it," Montoya shrugged. He flicked his hand at the wrist, and the signal was given. The encircling forces attacked the five defenders of the queen's honor.

Echoes once more reverberated around the plaza, but this time it was not the scream of a woman, but the clash of steel upon steel. The five defenders had formed a tight circle shoulder to shoulder with blades out-wards. All, including the lady of the court, wielded fine blades. While their skill and experience varied they were equally determined. At first the sheer fact of a dozen foes seemed to overwhelm them, but the captain and the musketeer's fought side by side in a fury that felled attacker after attacker. At their feet lay several bodies and irrespective of which uniform they wore their blood mingled into a single indistinguishable stream of red flowing across the cobble stones.

As they pressed their advantage on one aspect, The Spaniard pressed his on the other focusing on the courier and the lady.

"Hold!" Montoya's voice broke through the melee. "I have the prize. Drop your swords."

The combatants from all sides turned in the direct from which the command had originated. There stood Colonel Montoya with the courier La Porte, in his grasp. The brave messenger was once more disheveled, a gash in the arm of his tunic from which blood freely flowed. His leather document case on the floor by his feet. Montoya held a knife to his throat. Nudging the case with his foot the Spaniard indicated to Athos. "It looks like I have you at a disadvantage my dear Count. Open the case and hand me the queen's letter or I slice this man's throat."

Athos dropped his sword to the ground and walked towards the case. Dropping to one knee he withdrew a short knife and cut the straps of the case. Inserting his hand he slowly removed the folded parchment of a sealed letter. "So much trouble over so little." The musketeer stood, and as he started to hand the paper over, suddenly drew his arm backward and pitched it in the direction of Aramis stood behind him. The flying missive was instantly skewered on the tip of Aramis's sword. With a few flicks of the wrist it was reduced to shreds before the eyes of the incredulous Spaniard.

"What have you done? The Cardinal and I must have that letter."

"What letter is that?" Madame de Cheveuse asked demurely, "I know of no letter."

Athos smiled at the Spanish colonel. "You don't have a letter, we don't have a letter, it never existed. That's what we call detente my friend."

Finis

Notes on Noblesse Oblige

Texas - 2018

*J*honestly think my first conscious recollection of the *Three Musketeers* was the animated episodes that appeared as inserts in the Saturday morning psychedelic kids show of the late 1960s, *Banana Splits*. This was closely followed by the 1973 movie version starring Michael York, Oliver Reed, Frank Finlay, and Richard Chamberlin, and when I walked out of the cinema I was hooked. Over the ensuing years I think I've tracked down and watched every English language movie version of Dumas' classic story. And of course there were the books. I've read and reread the three novels, both full and abridged versions multiple times - although I will confess that my favorite Dumas tale is *The Count of Monte Cristo*.

The chance to play in the world of these classic swordsmen was an opportunity too good to pass up, but what story to tell. It turns out the gap between the setting of the *Three Musketeers* and its follow up novel, *Twenty Years Later* coincides with the historical events of the early stages of the Franco-Spanish war, which seemed like a perfect back drop for some action. While doing some research reading I came across a note that Anne, the Queen of France, was known to have undertaken a secret correspondence with her brother, Philip IV, the King of Spain. Apparently the correspondence went "beyond the requirements of sisterly affection," and she fell under such suspicion that the all powerful Cardinal Richelieu had her investigated. I had my story.

Anne's favorite courier for transporting the potentially treasonous missives was actually named LaPorte, although his fastidiousness and dislike of dogs is all my invention. In late 1637 Anne admitted her guilt and her movements were restricted, she was never allowed to be alone, and her household staff was purged and replaced by people loyal to the Cardinal.

Another character that was running around in my head was Dumas' father, Thomas-Alexander Dumas. A few years ago I read the biography[1] of this astonishing man who was, and remains, one of the highest ranking black officers in any European army and was the first general of color in

---

1   *The Black Count: Glory, Revolution, Betrayal, and the Real Count of Monte Cristo* - by Tom Reiss - 2012

the French Army until his popularity with the troops started to rival that of Napoleon, and he was quietly removed and written out of history. The time frames don't work for fitting him into the world of the musketeers, but he became the inspiration and model for Marc-Ange, the cardinal's man with the heart of a musketeer. After I had started this story further research unearthed mentions of at least one historical musketeer of color.

Rounding out the story in Toulouse was a nod to an early part of my professional career in aerospace when I was involved with the Airbus project and used to be in Toulouse on a regular basis. The Place du Capitole is still a magnificent open space where the local seat of government has been located since 1190, although the buildings have changed and evolved over the centuries. One part that still survives from the original medieval buildings is the Henri IV courtyard, and it was here that Richelieu did indeed have the popular Duke de Montmorency executed, a little nugget I've been carrying around in my head since I first stood on that spot nearly thirty years ago. And if you want to use a fact about Richelieu in a story, what better story setting is there to do that than one involving the Musketeers?

ALAN J. PORTER - Writer, and award-winning editor, Alan J. Porter, has written adventures featuring Sherlock Holmes, Allan Quatermain, Houdini, and private eye Rick Ruby; as well as his own New Pulp adventurers, The Raven and The Lotus Ronin. His pop-culture non-fiction work has featured properties such as Batman, Star Trek, The Beatles, and James Bond. He has also written comics for Tokyopop, BOOM Studios, Marvel, Disney, and Kid Domino.

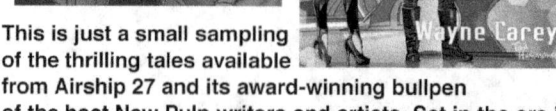